THE SEARCH FOR AMARA

Thank for your support

THE SEARCH FOR AMARA

A TEEN SERIES

INKED BY

JANAE M. ROBINSON

Love you! May God bless you! Enjoy!

Janae M Robinson

A TEEN SERIES

Copyright 2016 Janae M. Robinson

Edited By: Brandi Jefferson

Cover Designed by Aija Monique of AMB Branding

Published by Diamante' Publications, LLC

www.diamantepublications.com

THE SEARCH FOR AMARA

LETTER TO READERS:

The book was inked because I have a pre-teen that does not have books that she can read and relate to. The teen series that are out at this present time she has already read, and the books that are on the more advanced reading level that she reads on, are too mature for her to read. Dealing with teenagers on my job, at the church, and having my own have made me aware of a lot of the details that are going on in their world. Being in my thirties, I can say that some of the things that teens are doing and experiencing now are not how they were when we were teens. I ask that if you are an adult, you read this story with an open mind. Don't think oh this girl is too young to be doing this or that, because the reality is this is exactly what some twelve, thirteen, and fourteen year olds are doing or experiencing. No not all, but you would be surprised by what this generation is experiencing and experimenting with simply because no one is paying attention. Teens, read this story as a lesson learned. Yes this is fiction, but you must get out of the mindset of that it won't happen to me, that it doesn't happen in real life. Your age group is killing, being killed, getting kidnapped, being sold into sex trafficking, and much more. Technology gives way too much access and freedom. Stop sharing your personal information with strangers, posting all of your business, and arguing with people on social media. Teens, you are the future. We need you here to make this world continue. Set goals and strive to be the best that you can be. Stop comparing yourselves, stop competing, start encouraging, start building each other up, and help each other. Thank you for your support, and enjoy!

PROLOGUE

This cannot be how the rest of her years of high school are going to be, was the thought running through her mind. Amara laid in the hospital bed trying to remember what happened the night before. The last complete detail that Amara remembered was being at a party with her friends. Amara had gone through a period of rebellion when she had disrespected everyone, so her mother had totally revoked all overnight privileges. She was allowed to go hang out with her friends, but she was not allowed to spend the night for a while. When she finally got her sleepover privileges back, Amara took full advantage. Every chance she got, her and her friends would sneak out and go to a party. She remembered arriving at the party with her friends, and that was it. It was weird that Amara could remember almost everything that ever happened in her life except last night. It seem like hours had gone by and nobody, had been in her room. No nurse, no doctors, not even her mother. Just as Amara reached to push the call button, her mother and an older gentleman that obviously was the doctor entered in the room with unreadable expressions on their faces. Amara wished she could pretend to be sleep, but she really wanted some answers about what was going on.

CHAPTER ONE

Amara's family was in a good place in their lives. Her mother had been through so much over the years and finally she had her peace, but lately things seemed to be tense between Amara's mother and stepfather, Dwayne. He was one of Amara's favorite people other than her grandparents and of course her mother. Amara was happy that everything was going smooth, but she was terrified to be starting at a new high school without any of her friends that she had grown up with. Amara was aware that she would have to make some adjustments. One thing that she had learned that she was not prepared for was the strict dress code she would have to follow at the academy. A few weeks ago at orientation, she was shocked to find out her classmates had access to accounts that had more money in them than most of the teachers' yearly salaries. Amara decided that even with dress code, she was going to have to bring her 'A' game. The girls came to orientation with thousand dollar shoes and purses, and the boys came with diamonds blinging either on their wrist or their necks. Earrings were strictly prohibited for the young men. After orientation, Asha, Amara's mom was scheduled to take her to their bi-weekly salon visit. Dwayne showed up in her place which Amara found strange, but she kept her thoughts to herself. Amara's hairstylist kept her hair on point at all times. Amara had been begging her mother to get her hair cut, but the answer was always no. Amara had been going to the shop ever since she was seven. It was an every other Saturday event for her and her mother.

The only time scissors were allowed by her hair was to trim her ends. Since the girls in her class had grown up with her at her previous school, they knew that the hair that fell to the top of her butt was all hers. Amara started worrying again about what would the girls at her new school think, and how would they act.

After three hours, Dwayne was back to pick her up with DJ, her baby brother was asleep in the backseat. Amara and Dwayne rode in silence. She didn't even bother to ask where her mother was at. Pulling up to their mini mansion, Amara had to admit she got a little worried when she didn't see her mother's car. Without a word she got out of the car and went in the house.

Amara passed the kitchen and went straight up the stairs to her bedroom. She had been in a rush this morning, so she started cleaning up the small mess she had left behind. While she was putting away miscellaneous items off of her dresser she heard her mother shouting. *What now,* she thought. Stuck, she stood in one spot torn about what to do.

She wanted to go downstairs, but she didn't want to get dragged into the middle of an argument. Instead of going downstairs, Amara placed the items on the dresser, crossed over to her bed, and picked up her tablet. She couldn't believe that not only would she not be going to school with her friends, but since they moved she was now also about 45 minutes away from them. She loved how enormous her room was, but Amara would give it all up to be back with her friends. Scrolling through Instagram, she was getting teary eyed. She said a silent prayer because she didn't know how she was going to survive. Amara was sure she would eventually make it through, but she was not ready for the first few days of school.

Finally the voices quieted down, but then the door slammed so hard Amara felt the floor shake underneath her feet. Before Amara could make it to her door, Dwayne appeared carrying DJ. He looked very tired and frustrated. Amara felt bad for him and wish she knew what was going on with her mother.

"Hey 'Mara, get ready for bed. Your mom is upset, but you know she will be back in the morning. Asha would not miss out on your big first day of high school."

"You're right," Amara replied while hugging both Dwayne and DJ.

***

Amazingly Asha was not back in the morning. Dwayne got up and got DJ dressed while Amara changed her uniform three different times before finally being satisfied with her look. Leaving the house with just a little time to spare, Dwayne quickly maneuvered through traffic to get DJ to daycare first. Amara's school was closer to his job. Pulling in front of the daycare center, Amara quickly unfastened DJ and passed him over to Dwayne while kissing his cheeks. Dwayne ran in and asked DJ's teacher to please sign DJ in, so that he could get Amara to school on time. Speed walking into a slight jog Dwayne hopped in the car and was surprised to see Amara still sitting in the backseat.

"Amara are you coming up front?"

"No, I'm good."

"Ooookay" Dwayne responded deciding not to take it any further, but he knew what Amara was trying to do.

Amara was silent, but she had been on Instagram all morning and Sky, a young lady she had met at orientation had been posting as the students pulled up to the school. Dwayne had a black on black Tahoe, so she wasn't ashamed to pull up, but she was trying to portray an image so she would step out of the back of the car.

"Amara are you listening to me?"

"I'm sorry Dwayne, I zoned out, what did you say?"

"Yeah obviously! I was saying try to get in contact with your mom or grandmother, I can't come get you. Your mother must have forgotten I'm flying out this afternoon and won't be back until the end of the week."

"Oh ok. I will contact my grandma. What about DJ?"

"Delilah is keeping him for me."

"Wait a minute, what is really going on D? I'm a big girl, you can tell me."

"Amara this is a grown folk's situation, but all is well. You just worry about your image. I will even come around and open your door," Dwayne announced while putting the car in park.

Amara glanced up, shocked that they were sitting in front of the new school already. It looked like the red carpet event at an awards show. Dwayne came around as promised and opened her door. Amara smoothed down her skirt and stepped out of the truck. Her grandparents had bought her a Kate Spade backpack and her mother bought her a Louis Vuitton Monogram purse. Gathering her items after she stepped out, Dwayne placed them in her hands and gave her a salute as she walked towards the entrance.

Amara tried best not to stare as she walked through the doors.

"AMARA!"

Turning around, she tried to find Sky's face in the crowd because no one else knew her name. Looking around caused her long hair to flow back and forth across her shoulders.

"She trying to act like them bundles is her hair, GIRL BYE!"

Amara glanced into the face she had just seen plastered on her television last night. The girl's parents were part of a stupid reality show.

"Oh hello Taj, yeah sorry I don't rock bundles hun."

"Amara dang why are you so late?" Sky interjected and asked.

Taj glared at Amara but didn't know what to say. Most girls were either intimidated by her or worshipped her. *Who is the new chic,* Taj wondered.

"Sky I got up little late."

No way was Amara going to share that her mother had not come home last night. Sky was a tenth grader, her dad was an entertainment lawyer and her mom was a big name judge. She promised Amara she was like none of the pampered princesses and princes at Westbourne Academy. They had a few conversations over the phone since orientation. Sky was determined to tell all that she knew and keep Amara away from the troublemakers. Amara however was always her own person, and she would not let Sky's opinions stop her from at least being cordial.

"Oh ok, you got your schedule? I'm quite sure we won't have any classes together though."

Amara tried to keep a straight face. Sky had no idea that Amara had tested out of all the ninth grade classes, except biology. That class didn't have the test out option, but the other classes she passed the test and received the credit; another advantage that would lead her to Columbia University even sooner. A benefit Amara looked forward to, especially with all the craziness going on around her. She would be sad to leave her grandmother and DJ, but happy to be away. Sky took her schedule and looked at her with a confused expression. "Um, Amara you have to go to the office, these are tenth grade classes." Amara couldn't help but to laugh. "Sky, those are the right classes." "Girl say swear, oh so you really are smart! Oh well let's go, we have first period together." Amara stuffed her schedule down in her purse, put her backpack on her shoulder, and followed Sky down the hall.

CHAPTER TWO

Amara's first day of school was pretty uneventful. Her mother never responded to her text, but her grandmother had been there to pick her up.

"Chile is the pope in there or something?"

"No granny why you say that?"

"Look around, you don't see all of that security?"

"Oh granny that's because most of these children come from celebrity homes, remember?"

"Oh yes, I don't know why yo momma and Dwayne put you over here; spending all of that dang on money. Well I should say wasting, but I guess this school will look better on your college application."

Amara and her grandmother engaged in small talk all the way home. Pulling in the driveway, Amara was confused as to why her mom's car was in her grandparent's garage.

"Honey don't ask me no questions, go talk to your mother."

Amara didn't have to say a word; it was like her granny was reading her mind. She was hesitating to get out the car, because she was terrified of what this talk with her mother would reveal.

"Mara honey, get out of the car. Your mother is waiting inside for you."

Amara climbed out of the car, but immediately started a prayer in her head.

THE SEARCH FOR AMARA

Dear Lord, please hear my cry and let this talk be something positive and that my mommy will be coming home tonight. Lord we have been through so much already. Lord please just give us peace. In Jesus name, amen.

By the time Amara finished praying she was standing in the kitchen. She had to stifle a scream because she did not remember walking across the backyard, through the patio door and through the house to get to the kitchen.

"Asha come downstairs, your daughter is waiting for you."

Amara took a seat at the island in the middle of the kitchen. She loved coming to her grandparents' house because the stools had backs on them, so she didn't have to worry about slipping off. After a few minutes her mother finally walked into the kitchen.

"Hi baby, how was school?"

"My first day was great," Amara said clasping her hands together with obvious irritation.

Amara had to bite the inside of her cheek to stop herself from lashing out. She couldn't believe that her mother was about to sit here and act like nothing was going on. They continued to sit in silence, and although Amara could sense her mother's presence of fear she had no remorse.

"Mom."

"Amara baby."

The both suddenly started talking at the same time. Amara stopped and slightly nodded her head letting her mother know to keep talking.

"Amara, I know you are very smart so I will not beat around the bush. Dwayne and I are going through a rough patch. No worries though, I have been speaking with the first lady and she is praying for us."

Amara was relieved to know that her mom and stepdad were working through their issues.

"Great mom, I have homework. Are we staying here or going home?"

"No questions?"

"No you explained everything."

"Ok, so really how was your first day?"

"I survived!"

"Ok, well you can you start your homework, we will be going home in a couple of hours."

Amara went back out to her grandmother's car to get her backpack. Coming back in the house, Amara went down to the basement. Pulling out her Chromebook, she powered it on, and pulled out her books. Amara's phone started ringing just as she was logging into her classes. She was upset that she forgot to turn the ringer off. Pulling the phone out she glanced at the screen and had to answer when she saw it was her cousin Lace.

"Hey girl!" Amara answered while pulling up her classes to start her assignments.

"Amara how was school?"

"It was ok for the first day. One of the stuck up girls tried me. I checked her though and didn't have any more problems."

"That's right, get them in check early. I was calling to tell you about my mother. Girl she is driving me crazy. Now I see why my father killed himself."

"LACE, do not say that ever again. What is wrong with you?"

"I'm sorry Amara, but you just don't understand."

Amara and Lace talked for another 20 minutes before Amara had to end the call to finish her homework. Amara had a lot of thoughts going through her mind. She had to refocus so she could finish her homework. When she finally finished, she cleaned off the table and started her way upstairs.

Walking into the living room, she was happy to see her mother ready to go. Her mother's bags were neatly stacked by the door with her purse sitting on top. Amara wondered how long her mother had planned to stay away.

Instead of voicing her thoughts, Amara asked "Mom are you ready to go?"

"Just a few more minutes' sweetie, I want to see the end of this movie."

"Ok, I will be upstairs talking to granny."

"That's fine," Asha responded pulling her phone out of her jacket pocket.

Amara was confused when a huge smile spread across her mother's face, but she turned to go find her grandmother.

***

Amara was happy to finally be at home in her bed. She really just wanted to pass out, but she had to gather her clothes for the next day and take a shower. She popped up quickly before she went to sleep.

After taking longer in the shower than she had planned, Amara rushed to put on her pajamas so she could call Dwayne. Putting her things away and getting out her clothes for the next day, she was interrupted when her phone started ringing.

One day I am going to remember to turn the ringer off when I'm busy, Amara thought.

"Hello," she answered without even noticing who the caller was.

"Girl, how did you make an enemy on your first day?"

"Sky, what are you talking about?"

"You haven't been on Instagram or Facebook today?"

"No, I had homework. Stop being so evasive and tell me what is going on."

"E what? There you go with your big words. Anyway Taj is telling everyone that she checked you today and how you were lying about rocking weave saying that weave was ratchet!"

"What, she is crazy! I didn't even talk to her long enough to say all of that."

"Yes, we know that but be prepared to have some nasty looks tomorrow."

Amara was ready to get off the phone. She was not in the mood to deal with or hear anymore drama. She was starting to wish she would have just kept her mouth closed.

"Sky I will see you tomorrow, my mother is calling me."

"Ok, meet me in front of the school."

"Ok," Amara said and ended the call.

What have I gotten myself into? Amara thought.

Amara was still standing in the middle of the floor where she stopped when she answered the phone. Remembering that she was had to get out her clothes and wanted to call Dwayne before she went to bed, Amara started moving quickly. Pulling out a skirt and a blouse for tomorrow, she carefully placed both items across the back of the chair at her desk. Amara took one last look around making sure that everything was in its proper place and all electronics were turned off, she finally got in her bed with her cell phone.

Amara thought she had dialed Dwayne's number, so she was shocked when she heard her grandmother's voice.

"Hey Mara sugar, is everything okay?"

"Yes granny. Actually I was trying to call Dwayne; I don't know how I dialed you."

"Well tell me what is troubling your spirit baby."

"Huh? I'm not troubled."

"Amara now you know you cannot outsmart your granny."

Amara realized that her grandmother was right and started explaining to her what had happened between her and Taj, and that she had just got off the phone with Sky who warned her about possible drama tomorrow. Her grandmother asked did Sky ever do anything besides spread gossip, and told Amara that she might need to steer clear of her.

Thinking about what her granny had just said, Amara reached over for her tablet and started scrolling on Facebook. She was shocked to see that Taj had indeed made a post that had 293 comments under it. Amara clicked on the comments and started reading, it seemed like Sky was trying to play both sides. Reading comments from girls that she didn't even know who were threatening to cut her hair when they saw her, really had Amara terrified. Instantly Amara felt sick, she started yawning so she could get off the phone. "Amara you don't have to fake being sleepy with me lil girl, goodnight and remember what I told you about that Sky girl." "Ok, Goodnight granny, I love you." Amara ended another call feeling anxious and uncertain. She was not sure what was going to happen tomorrow but she was sure that it was going to be something bad. She decided that she would call Dwayne in the morning before school.

CHAPTER THREE

The next morning Amara woke up and started getting dressed. She decided to be on the safe side and put her hair up in a bun just in case one of the girls wanted to make good on their threats to cut her hair. Amara knew that she was supposed to just pray and let God fight her battles, but being a teenager that was a hard concept.

"Amara are you ready?" Asha called up the stairs.

Amara forgot that her little brother was not here, so her mother would be moving faster than normal. Asha had a nice Lexus truck, but Amara still wished that she was pulling up in Dwayne's Tahoe. She took a final glance in the mirror making sure that everything was in place. She smoothed down the front of her skirt, sprayed oil sheen, and brushed up her hair.

"Here I come mommy."

Lord please get me through this day.

Amara said a quick silent prayer in her head as she ran down the stairs.

She grabbed a banana and a bottle of water out of the refrigerator on her way out the door.

"Amara is everything ok?"

"Of course mommy," Amara responded while taking a swig of water.

Asha pulled up to the school and was amazed by the scene in front of her. The young girls were looking like grown women with weave flowing down their back, lashes curled inches away from their face, and thousand dollar purses on their arms. One girl walked past the car with four inches heels on that Asha was sure she had seen in a magazine for $5,000.

"Where do these kids' parents work?" Asha asked.

"Most of their parents are celebrities. The girl that I had run in with yesterday, her parents has a reality show."

"You had a run in yesterday?"

Dang it, I forgot I didn't tell her! Amara thought.

"Yes mother, nothing major though I took care of it."

"Amara be careful and stay out of trouble."

"Ok" Amara replied while getting out of her car.

Amara looked through the crowd and didn't see Sky anywhere. Turning around she was relieved to see that her mother's car was no longer in view. Pulling out her phone to call Sky, she was surprised when it was knocked out of her hand.

"I see you were smart enough to put that hair up, you better watch your back!" a tall girl Amara had never seen before yelled in her face, before placing some scissors back in her book bag.

Amara slowly picked her phone up off the ground, crossed the street, and enter the school building. She decided she would just see Sky in class.

Totally bypassing her locker and going straight to class, it felt like her heart would burst clear out of her chest. Amara had never been in a fight, threatened, or even in an argument before. To say that she was scared would be an understatement, terrified would be better description.

Right before the bell rang, Sky walked into the classroom like she was waiting for the cameras to start flashing. Amara sat perfectly still full of irritation.

"Where were you this morning?"

Sky walked to the middle of the classroom and pretended that she didn't even hear Amara.

"Sky I know you heard me!"

"Amara the bell has rung, please pull out your notebook and complete the Do Now on the board" Mrs. Loy, the homeroom teacher instructed.

Amara did as the teacher said but she couldn't believe that Sky was ignoring her. She finished the assignment in five minutes and just stared Sky down while everyone else was finishing their work.

"Excuse me Amara, are you having difficulties?"

"With what Mrs. Loy?"

"The assignment on the board."

"No ma'am."

"Well stop staring at the back of your classmates' heads and get busy."

Loud snickering erupted around the classroom, with some of the class turning to look at Amara.

"Mrs. Loy I am finished."

"What? No way!"

"Yes I am would you like me to bring it up to you?"

"Sure thing, and if I find out you cheated you will be going home for a few days."

"Now how do you suppose that I cheated, no one else is finished."

Mrs. Loy snatched the paper out of Amara's hand and pulled her answer key out of her top drawer. The assignment stated that it would take students at least 30 minutes to complete and that is why she had given it to the class.

Mrs. Loy was at a loss for words. Not only were all the answers correct, but Amara had shown the work as well.

"Amara, I need to see you after class."

The class started whispering and laughing because they just knew that Amara was in trouble. Amara knew that she was not, but she was thankful for the disruption in her day. She was thinking about calling her grandmother to come get her, something in her spirit was telling her that today was going to be full of trouble.

Glancing towards the front of the class, she noticed that Sky shifted her attention the other way quickly.

Finally the bell rang, dismissing the class. Sky kept her head down while she hurried past Amara and out the classroom. Again Amara got a heavy feeling that someone bad was going to happen before the day was over. Once everyone was out of the classroom, Mrs. Loy started asking Amara how was she able to complete the problems so quickly and what major did she plan to study in college. After having a heart to heart conversation Mrs. Loy made sure that Amara understood that she was truly gifted and had a bright future. Amara promised that she knew who she was and she would not let her peers influence her. By the time they were finished talking, Amara had missed her second period class and it was time for her to go to lunch. She was regretting this period and wished that she could miss it. Westbourne did not play that, they had a zero tolerance policy for any students being in the hallway. Mrs. Loy didn't have a second period class that's how they talked through that class, but the students were starting to come in now so Amara had to go to lunch.

CHAPTER FOUR

The cafeteria was extremely loud today. Sky had already schemed up enough lies to ensure a fight, or at least an argument. She had been telling Taj all night through Kik lies about Amara. Taj and her crew were looking for a fight. Poor Amara had no idea what she was about to walk into.

Sky was very conniving. Taj was angry, Amara was clueless, and Sky was nowhere to be found. Sky made sure that she sat in the back of the cafeteria behind a large crowd so that she was not seen, but she could see what was going on.

Amara walked into the cafeteria and looked around at all the different cliques sitting at the tables. It seemed like all the students counted for in the school were all at lunch this period. A calm silence swept over the cafeteria when Amara entered the line to get some hot wings.

Taj and her crew strutted across the cafeteria and approached Amara as she finished placing her order. She looked over her shoulder and kept moving like they were not even in her space.

"Don't look scared now bitch! What was all the shit you were talking to your little friend?"

Amara smiled and kept right on about her business.

"Oh so now you can't hear?"

Amara still ignored her because her grandmother had always told her it is not what they call you, but what you answer to.

Suddenly Taj grabbed Amara and that is when Amara responded while snatching away.

"Do not touch me. If you want to talk to me, my name is Amara!"

"Little girl I do not give a damn what your name is! You had a mighty mouth when talking to your girl Sky, let me hear it."

Amara couldn't believe that everyone had gathered as close as possible to make sure they were part of the action. She laughed to herself, because her classmates were not going to get the show they were looking for. She was always taught to conduct herself appropriately in public.

"Taj, I don't know what Sky told you. However it is obvious that she is not my friend. So whatever you THINK I said, I guarantee you that I did not. I do not hide behind technology. Sky called me and told me about your post on Facebook. I also saw that she was on there kissing your behind. I don't hang with people like that."

Taj just stood there confused, she really didn't know what to believe. Sky never had talked to her before and she did think it a little strange that the first person she had ever seen Sky hanging with was now the person she was talking about.

"Taj don't believe that, she is just scared," a voice came from one of Taj's friends.

"Naw, I'm going to let her slide this time, but bitch I advise you not to let my name slip from your lips again."

"Again my name is not bitch. I never have a reason to speak your name unless I am speaking to you. Just make sure you give me that same respect please and thank you."

The crowd looked on in shock because no one ever stood up to Taj, NO ONE!

Amara paid for her purchase and looked around for somewhere to sit. She saw Sky sitting way in the back away from everyone but with a clear view of what had just happened obviously by the look on her face. Amara walked over and sat right next to her.

"Hey why have you been acting so weird today?"

Sky wasn't sure how to respond, she had not expected Amara to speak to her.

"Ummm I don't know."

"Wow Sky really that's all you have to say is you don't know?"

"Amara want do you want me to say?"

"Well you can start with why you would tell Taj lies about me."

Sky wished that she had the courage that Amara had. First she had stood up for herself against Taj, and now she was confronting her in a calm tone. Sky was so embarrassed. Last year she didn't have any friends because her parents weren't some famous celebrities, and the information that she was there on a scholarship got leaked and spread throughout the whole school.

THE SEARCH FOR AMARA

When Amara came to orientation, Sky was excited to see another girl in the school who had ordinary, non-famous parents. Sky thought this would be her great opportunity to create a friend and fill her mind with nonsense so she wouldn't want to be around the other girls in the school.

Over the summer, Sky pumped Amara's head with a little truth and a lot of lies, especially about the popular girls that had shunned her during her freshman year. She thought her planned had worked so well until Amara had a run in with Taj; now the whole school was talking about the new girl that had put Taj in her place.

That small incident had created a large amount of jealousy in Sky, which led her to try to make the girls flat out hate Amara. She thought her planned had worked until a few moments ago when Amara had stood up for herself once again, gaining the respect of everyone who witnessed the events.

"Look Sky I know what you were trying to do, I am just trying to figure out why? I thought we were friends."

"Amara I'm sorry. I got upset because you aren't scared of Taj and she knows it. I thought you would become her friend and start ignoring me."

"Really? I am not that type of person, but you really need to stop gossiping and telling lies. Or you are right; you will not have any friends!"

As the girls finished up their talk, the bell alerted them that their lunch hour was up and it was time to get to their next class. U.S. History was their next class that they shared together. As they walked through the cafeteria, Amara noticed the stares but chose to ignore them.

Amara always found U.S. History boring because they didn't teach her about her history, but today the lesson was actually interesting. Mr. Rankins, the teacher passed out a U.S. History timeline and instructed the students to select a period and do a five page research paper about it. They had to have at least six resources and the assignment was due in two weeks

Sky turned around with a look of panic on her face and mouthed the words *HELP ME.* Amara had to cover her mouth to keep from screaming out with laughter. Sky was being dramatic; this was not a difficult assignment.

During the rest of the class, the teacher was trying to get the students to brainstorm out loud plans for their assignment. Amara seemed to be the only one talking and she couldn't believe how hard her peers were trying to make the assignment seem.

Mr. Rankins stopped, looked over the class and asked, "Does anyone have any questions, because nobody is talking except Amara?"

Everybody just shook their heads and the bell rang dismissing the class.

Mr. Rankins assured Amara on her way out that she was on the right track and he looked forward to reading her paper.

Amara agreed to meet Sky this weekend at the library to help her and then walked off to her next class. The day flew by quickly, and now Amara was standing outside waiting for her mother to pull up.

Glancing down at her phone texting her mom, she didn't notice the boy who had walked up and was staring at her in admiration. Immediately she felt her face turning red.

"Hey Miss Lady, what is the name of the wonderful self-assured girl that takes no junk?"

Amara had to cover her mouth, she felt herself grinning like a fool. She had first noticed this fine boy at orientation, and she couldn't believe that he was now in her face asking her name.

"My name is Amara, what is your name?"

"Tay."

"Is that what is on your birth certificate?"

"Oh you just love being smart I see, my name is Dontay."

"Well nice to meet you Dontay. I am not being smart; I just want to know your full name."

"So you must not be from around here, because everybody around here kisses Taj's behind."

"Everybody? Does that include you?"

"No, I guess I should have said all the girls."

"Well no I am not from around here, but if I was I do not kiss behinds or play follow the leader. I stand on my own two feet and focus on being Amara."

The two continued conversing back and forth, making sure to exchange numbers so that they could talk later on. Asha pulled up, smashing the brakes and hopping out the car.

"Get your fast tail in the car and out of that boy's face. This is not where you are supposed to be waiting for me."

Amara couldn't believe her mother was acting like this. Asha's eyes were red and she reeked of liquor. Amara was glad to see that Dontay had made his exit and even more excited that she had gotten his number.

"Mom I was not being fast," Amara responded while walking to the car and rolling her eyes.

"Yeah whatever, let's go. I'm dropping you off with your brother."

"Why? Can I go to my granny's?"

"Don't back talk me; you heard what I just said!"

Amara sat back and closed her eyes trying to calm her nerves. Her mother was acting crazy and she knew that she couldn't stand being at Delilah's house. Amara's eyes flew open.

"Is Dwayne going to be there?"

"I don't know! Don't ask me about him and do not call your grandmother. I will be back at the end of the week to pick you and your brother up."

"Wait a minute, the end of the week! How am I going to get to school?"

"Delilah will take you, don't worry about it."

"Mom you know I do not like Delilah."

"You better watch your mouth young lady!"

"But mo--"

"Don't but mom me, you are going over there. That is final. Delilah will take you to school and her driver will pick you up after school. I have already made all of the arrangements."

Amara was so angry she couldn't stop the tears from flowing. She tried to look on the bright side that at least her brother and little cousins would be there, but she really had a strong dislike for Delilah. After all what kid wouldn't when they heard someone totally dogging their mother out behind her back?

Amara wiped her face and stared out the window. She felt her phone vibrating in her purse, but she dared not even look at it just in case it was Dontay. She would be with Lace in a few more minutes and she would check her notifications then. "Ok, they are waiting for you. If you have an emergency call me, otherwise I will call you this weekend." "Where are you going?" "To take care of business, now go they are waiting for you," Asha said while pointing at the door where Lace was standing holding DJ. "Wait mom, I don't have any clothes!" Asha pushed the button to open the gate so Amara could get her duffle bag with her clothes in it. Amara grabbed her purse and backpack, stepped out the car and slammed the door while stomping to the rear of the car. Lace had placed DJ down inside the door and came out to help Amara. Asha was so fed up she pulled off without even saying goodbye. The girls just shared a look and went into the house.

CHAPTER FIVE

"Girl what is going on with our mothers?" Lace asked while walking up the stairs.

Amara was so into playing with her brother that she didn't even hear Lace speaking. It had been days although it felt like weeks since she had last seen DJ. She was starting to feel like something big was going on, and she was determined to figure it out soon.

"Amara are you listening to me?" Lace asked again.

Lace had been talking for quite some time and Amara still had yet to answer or even acknowledge the fact that she was speaking.

"Sorry Lace, it has been so long since the last time I held DJ, now what were you saying?"

"I was just talking about how both of our mothers are acting strange like they are hiding some type of secrets, and my mother keeps talking crazy."

"Crazy like what Lace, what is she saying?"

"The other night she thought I was sleep, but I heard her talking to Melissa!"

"What? Melissa...Dwayne's Melissa?"

"The one and only!"

Amara tried to keep a straight face, but she suddenly started feeling sick and had to sit down with DJ. Melissa was the woman that had come and caused a ton of drama for both families. Asha had seen a wedding picture of Dwayne and Melissa, but later found out it was not a real wedding. However Dwayne did still cheat on Asha with Melissa.

"Well, I am not going to jump to any conclusions. Let me tell you what happened at school today."

Amara started explaining in vivid details everything that happened at school. Lace was listening with an intense expression on her face, hoping for Amara to finish soon so she could give her two cents without interrupting.

Amara paused to laugh at how DJ had fallen asleep, and Lace took that as an opportunity to interject.

"Amara, this Sky character sounds like nothing but trouble. You might want to stay away from her."

Before Amara could answer, her phone started ringing. Lace was extremely interested in who could possibly have her cousin smiling so hard.

Amara was trying to decide if she wanted to talk to Tay in front of Lace. She was going to send him to voicemail and just send him a text, but she decided to just go ahead and answer at the last minute.

"Hello."

"Hey Amara, are you busy?"

Amara felt butterflies flying around in her stomach. Dontay sound much older and sexier on the phone. She had to catch her breath before she could respond.

"Umm it depends on who I am talking to."

"Oh is that right? You got it like that, so many guys ringing your line?"

Amara felt so stupid! Trying to be cool had backfired in her face.

"No Tay, of course I don't I--"

"Amara calm down, it was a joke."

Dontay could hear the anxiety building up in Amara's voice, but he knew that she was not that type of girl. Matter of fact, everyone that had tried to get her number had failed. Dontay still wasn't sure why she had agreed to talk to him.

"Oh, sorry. I am not busy, what are you doing?"

Dontay and Amara laughed and talked while Lace stood in front of Amara continuously asking who Amara was talking to. Amara just smiled and kept holding up one finger signaling for her to wait.

Amara was enjoying her conversation but she knew that Lace would not give up until she received an answer.

"Tay, can I call you back in like 30 minutes?"

"I thought you weren't busy!"

"I know but--"

"Amara lighten up girl, I was joking...again."

"Oh ok"

"Just make sure you call me back."

"Oh most certainly."

"Alright, talk to you soon."

"Bye bye!"

Amara barely tapped the end option before Lace started attacking her with questions one after another. Stalling was not an option so Amara just started giving Lace all the details. It would be another two years before Lace got a chance to finally experience the high school life.

The girls laid across the bed while Lace continued to ask questions, like was Amara still a virgin?

Amara assured her that she was and that talking to Dontay would not change anything. Amara wanted to give Lace a health class type lesson about sex, but she knew that was not her place. Once Lace seemed satisfied with all of her questions, she began talking about her mother. Apparently from what Lace was saying, Amara gathered that Delilah had been in heavy communication with Melissa. They were talking long periods of time, multiple times a day. Amara started wondering if Melissa's name back in the picture had anything to do with Dwayne's absence. Amara felt a sense of irritation and didn't want to listen anymore. She pulled out her phone and sent Dontay a text message to see what he was doing. Waiting for him to respond, she decided to check her social media pages. Lace was still talking in the background, and Amara was nodding her head like she was listening.

CHAPTER SIX

The next day at school Amara felt like a celebrity. Everyone was speaking to her and now her name was known by all the popular people. Taj had even invited her to sit at their lunch table. Sky was back acting weird, but Amara determined that this time it was jealousy.

"So Amara what do your parents do?" Taj's friend Courtney asked.

"My mom is in the social work field, and my stepdad is the owner of a life insurance company."

"Oh that's so basic, so you must be here on a scholarship."

"COURTNEY!" Taj jumped up and shouted.

Amara just looked up and smiled while shaking her head. So now she had another girl once again to put in their place.

"You are right; my family is very...uh what did you call us basic? We are an example that you can have money without exploiting ourselves!"

Courtney's parents were known because of their third season of a couple's reality show that was utterly ridiculous and most people were shocked that it even still came on.

A loud eruption of laughter exploded shocking Amara; she didn't realize that anybody else had heard her. Taj and Courtney both sat with astonished looks. An awkward silence took over the table. Amara picked up her fruit cup and continued eating. She was actually getting tired of proving herself to these girls.

"Well, so um Amara there is a party this weekend. Would you like to go?"

Amara wanted to go, but she doubted if it would be possible. Her mother was gone who knows where and Delilah was definitely not going to let her go. She had to think of something quick.

"Sure, do you think I could spend the weekend at your house? I mean not trying to intrude, but it will be easier for my mother."

Amara couldn't believe that she just told a lie. She never lied to her friends or classmates unnecessarily.

"Of course, I was going to ask you that anyway," Taj responded with excitement.

Amara quickly came with a great idea. Her grandmother and Delilah didn't like each other, so they would never call each other. Amara would tell Delilah she was going over her grandmother's house for the weekend.

"Do you need my driver to come pick you up tonight or can your mom bring you?"

Awww man, Amara was thinking too quickly. She completely forgot she would have to go to Delilah's house to get clothes.

"Ummm…"

"Better yet just come over tonight, we can just go to the mall and get you something cute for tomorrow. I need something new anyway."

"Oh no, Taj I can't let you do that."

"You can and you will. I always take my friends shopping. Why do you think they hang with me? I am not stupid, but hey it's not my money and my parents have plenty. Plus your look has to be on fleek!! You will have competition with Dontay being there!"

Amara started blushing and cheesing at the same time, wondering how Taj knew about Tay.

"Oh you couldn't have thought Taj didn't have the scoop! I think you guys make a cute couple. You must be something special because he is an 11th grader and he has never talked to anyone here at the school. He and my brother are my best friends."

"You have a brother?"

"Yep. I know you're thinking why don't they mention him on the show. He made my parents sign a clause that states they can't mention him in the show. He attends an Ivy League school and doesn't want the spotlight or the drama following him."

"Wow! How do you feel about it?"

Taj and Amara talked until the bell rung signaling that lunch was ending. Amara had developed a completely different attitude about Taj. Apparently even though Taj would never come right out and say it, she was afraid and confused. Taj was in the tenth grade and last year she was barely known. This year with her parents being in the spotlight and her occasionally being on the show, she had gained unheard of popularity. Even some of the senior girls were part of her circle. Taj knew that mainly all of her friends stuck around her because of her money, and possibly having a chance to be on television.

The girls went their separate ways to class and agreed to meet up in front of the school at the end of the day. Amara sat in her Civics class trying to focus, but her mind was on so many things at once. A balled up piece of paper came flying from across the room and landed on her desk. Amara jumped and looked around to see who had thrown it. Everyone was either focused or had their heads down sleep. Amara didn't really know anybody in this class so she had no clue who threw the paper. Amara went back to all the distractions going on in her mind. She felt her phone vibrating in her purse, but decided to ignore it until later. The vibration stopped and started right back up. This time Amara pulled it partially out of her purse to look at the screen.

It was a number that she didn't recognize so she sent it voicemail. Before she could close her purse the vibration started again. Amara raised her hand and asked to be excused to go to the restroom.

Once she entered into one of the stalls in the bathroom, she pulled out her phone and called the number back. The phone connected and disconnected on the other end without anyone saying anything. Amara looked at the phone puzzled and started to dial the number back, but the phone started ringing.

"Hello," Amara answered quickly.

"Just listen I don't have long to talk. Stay away from Dontay and watch out. Everyone you think is your friend is not!"

The caller disconnected not leaving Amara a chance to say anything. She looked around the bathroom full of confusion. She had no idea who was calling her, or why they were issuing threats and warnings. Amara decided to go back to class and she would show Dontay the number later and see what he had to say.

Amara made it back to class right before it was over. A girl sitting in the front of the class caught Amara's eye, and rolled hers as if she was disgusted with her. The bell signaled dismal, and students rushed out of the classroom as it was getting closer to the end of the day.

Walking to her locker, Amara was pushed from behind and fell before she could catch her fall. Books, paper, her purse, and other belongings went scattering across the floor. The boys were laughing and the girls were just standing in astonishment.

"Get out of my way!" Dontay yelled while pushing through the crowd, "Amara are you ok? What happened?"

"Get away from me," Amara whispered while gathering her stuff off the floor so she could get up.

"What is wrong with you? What I do? I didn't push you," Dontay was hurt and confused.

Amara refused to answer him. She just got all of her stuff and stomped off in the direction to her next class. When she finally made it to a desk she fell in the chair and put her head down.

"Excuse me Miss Dawning; can I talk to Amara please?"

"Make it quick, my class is starting," Miss Dawning replied as the bell rang.

Amara didn't lift up her head because she didn't want to talk to Dontay, nor did she care what he had to say. She just wanted him to leave her alone and the day to hurry up and be over. She almost forgot that she was going home with Taj, and really wanted to just go curl up in her grandmother's bed. "Amara, please just listen to me. I don't understand why you are mad at me. I promise I have not done anything, but I need to know what is going on?" Dontay pleaded. "Listen here Casanova; you will have to worry about your love issues after school. Get to your class." Amara was thankful that Miss Dawning put Dontay out the class. In her opinion there was nothing to talk about. Dontay knew more than he was saying, guilt was all in his voice. Amara was not sure what was going on, but she was so over new drama every day. "Amara are you ok?" Miss Dawning asked. Amara picked up her head and just nodded. She reached down and pulled out her notebook and textbook. Looking up at the board, Amara tried to focus and copy down the notes. Once again her phone started vibrating. This time the phone showed a text message notification instead of a missed call. Opening the message after she noticed it was from the same number that had called, Amara was both amused and aggravated. The message read that whoever was harassing her was glad that she had listened to her instructions, and as long as she continued to stay away from Dontay everything would be ok. Amara could not understand why everyone kept picking with her. Sky had been M. I. A. all day, which made Amara think about the warning she had received. There was no time to worry about Sky though. It was one more class before the day was over, and then she would be in a house full of television cameras. Amara planned to make sure she stayed out the way. The last thing she needed was to be on TV.

CHAPTER SEVEN

The end of the school day finally came and Amara stood outside waiting for Taj. She ignored all the weird and crazy glances she kept getting. Amara really wanted to just yell at her classmates to stop looking at her like they had never seen someone fall before. Truthfully she didn't fall; she was pushed and still had no idea who was the guilty culprit.

The fall was definitely intentional. After Amara had went to class and thought about what happened, she vividly remembered being shoved before she hit the ground. She pulled out her phone and then remembered she didn't even have Taj's phone number. So instead of just standing around looking stupid, Amara took a seat and prayed that Taj would appear soon.

"Amara will you please just talk to me," Dontay said while sitting down next to her.

"Dontay what?"

"Thank you, that's a start!"

"What do you want? I have nothing to say to you."

"Amara, can you please just tell me what happened? Can I at least defend myself?"

"Dontay listen, I am a young girl that does not have time for nor will I put myself in grown folk type drama."

"Ok Amara, now I am totally lost. What are you talking about?"

Amara was getting frustrated, irritated, and ready for Taj to come out the building. She felt stupid that she didn't get Taj's number. As long as she had been sitting outside, there had not been a car to pull up and just sit. Amara was beginning to worry that Taj had left her.

"Ohhh man!" Amara jumped up and shouted.

She had completely forgotten to let Delilah know that she didn't have to come pick her up or send a driver. Amara hurried into the building so that if a car pulled up, she would not be seen. Walking swiftly down the hall with her head down texting, she didn't even notice anyone else in the building until she bumped into Courtney.

"Oops excuse me."

"Yeah you better watch your step around here."

"Nice, hey have you seen Taj?"

"Why would I tell you?"

"Ummm maybe because I asked you."

"You know you have a smart mouth. Don't think just cuz you stood up for yourself that you are that deal around here now. Taj is my best friend, and Tay had his eyes on me until you came on the scene. I warned you nicely to step off and I even tried to help you by telling you to steer clear of Sky."

Amara was shocked, but everything was coming together.

"So that was you calling and texting me?"

"Ding ding ding. You solved the mystery, now I am not going to give you anymore warnings!"

Courtney turned and jogged out of the school. Amara didn't know what to make out of what just happened. She felt like Taj had set her up, because obviously Amara had been left without a ride. The silence in the huge school was spooky, so Amara hurried back outside.

Seeing Dontay still sitting outside made her feel a little better. Amara still didn't plan on talking to him, but at least she wouldn't be waiting for her grandmother by herself.

"Why are you still here?"

Amara ignored him while dialing her grandmother's number and placing her phone up to her ear.

"Hi grandma," an eager Amara said as soon as the call was connected, "can you come pick me up from the school?"

Her grandmother gave her the third degree of why was she still at school and where was her mother. It had slipped Amara's mind that her mother told her not to tell her grandmother that she was gone. This is what happened when you didn't do what you were supposed to do. Things all started falling apart.

Trying to sneak around with Taj had gotten her left behind at school. Now she would have to think of another lie to tell her grandmother about why her mother couldn't come pick her up. Amara's grandmother was the type you could not just tell anything, she would dig and dig. She acted like detectives in an interrogation room! Finally she said she was on her way.

"Dang your grandmother sounds like she doesn't play! How did you miss your ride anyway?"

Amara just stared straight ahead like Dontay was not talking to her. She started trying to figure what was Taj's motive behind all of this. Taj was the one that had assured her that Dontay had never even talked to any of the girls in the school.

"Amara you are not being fair and you are acting very childish."

Amara bit the inside of her cheek to stop from responding, she wished her grandmother would hurry up. She stood up and starting walking down the street to get away from Dontay. He was really starting to get on her nerves. She really wanted to tell him what was going on, but she had a feeling he just wouldn't be honest.

Almost reaching the corner, finally she saw her grandmother coming up the street. Amara stopped walking and waited for her grandmother to pull up. Once the car came to a complete stop, Amara got in and tried to avoid her grandmother's intimidating stare.

"Amara where is your mother, and who is that boy watching your every move?"

"I don't know grandma," Amara tried to answer both questions indirectly, but she should have known better.

"You don't know what? Never mind! I will just call your mother and ask the little boy myself why is he watching you?"

Amara knew that she was either going to die from embarrassment or her mother was going to kill her.

"Excuse me young man, do you know my granddaughter?"

Amara tried to plead with her eyes for Dontay to say no, and just when she thought he had got the hint he started walking up to the car.

"Hello ma'am, I know Amara very well. We have classes together and I was just making sure she was safe while she was sitting out here."

Dontay was lying; they did not have any classes together. He was trying to get in good with her grandmother thinking maybe he would gain some ground back with Amara.

"Why thank you. That was very kind of you, do you need a ride?"

"No thank you, I have a ride."

"Ok, Amara say goodbye to your friend. Why would you say you don't know him? He was very kind to sit and wait with you."

Amara wished that looks could injure. She didn't want to kill Dontay, but she certainly wanted his lip to feel like he had gotten punched in the mouth.

"Goodbye," she responded through clenched teeth.

Dontay smiled as he started walking backwards away from the car.

Finally they were off to her grandmother's house. Amara put her head back and closed her eyes. She was trying to decide how exactly she was going to finish this day out. She hadn't really lied when she said she didn't know where her mother was. Her mother hadn't given her any information or even clues about where she was going.

Amara had cut her ringer back on, so the music blared through the quiet car. This was one reason she personalized ringtones, she knew that Lace was calling.

"Amara I know your phone ringing."

"Hello," Amara answered with an attitude.

"Dang girl what happened? My mother just told me you aren't coming back over."

"I am coming back, just not tonight."

"Oh no you are not young lady!" Amara's grandmother interrupted.

"Why not?"

"Who are you talking to? Little girl give me that phone," her grandmother said while snatching it out of her hand before she could even end the call.

"Grandma what is wrong with you?"

"What is wrong with me? No! What is wrong with you? You do not talk to me like that!"

Amara turned and looked out the window. She felt a little bad for yelling at her grandmother, but she was upset that her grandmother was not letting her go back with Lace or even talk to her. When her mother came home she was going to have a series of questions to answer. Tears started sliding down Amara's face and she really couldn't understand why.

Trying to be discreet with wiping away her tears, Amara wasn't quick enough for her grandmother.

"You know why you are crying?"

Amara just shook her head back and forth but refusing to look at her grandmother.

"Well that's because God is here."

Amara turned to her grandmother with her eyes bulged open, "What?"

"Yes child whenever tears start flowing and you don't know why, it is because you are in the presence of the Lord."

"Grandma that doesn't even make sense; God does not just pop up where we are. We are in a car, why would He come here? We weren't even singing or anything!"

"I knew that God would work it out for me to take you to this revival tonight. How about we go change our clothes, get something to eat and go to church?"

Amara really liked church. On Sunday mornings not Friday! However she knew that her grandma was being nice, but going was not up for question. Alicia didn't play with Asha when she was little, and she was not about to play with her granddaughter either. Whenever she went to church, if you were in her house, you didn't get a choice.

Finally they pulled up in the driveway. Amara opened the door to rush in the house to get ready to go. She planned to sneak and try to call Lace, and check Taj's page on Facebook. Before she was completely out of the car her grandmother stopped her.

"Amara listen. I know right now a lot is going on, but you don't get to take it out on me. I know that your mom is gone, but you will be ok. I am going to keep you here with me. I will call Delilah tonight and let her know that she can bring DJ also. If it is ok with her, you both can go over there on the weekends until whenever your mother finds her way back home. Deal?"

"That sounds great grandma. Thank you!"

Amara was so happy that she would still get to be around Lace. She loved Lace, but truthfully she did not want to deal with Delilah on an everyday basis. The biggest bonus was getting DJ back with her every night.

***

Amara and her grandmother pulled up to the church, and Amara was surprised to see how many cars were parked in the parking lot.

"Grandma what is the theme for this revival? It is a lot of cars here."

Amara had grown up in the church and she knew that her pastor did not do anything without a theme. Her mother had been brought up in the church as well, so Amara was surprised that her mother hadn't been talking about an upcoming revival.

"This revival's theme is 'Time to Fight'"

A look of confusion came across Amara's fight. She didn't get why a church would be telling people that it is time to fight. Wasn't that against Christian behavior? Her grandmother just laughed and grabbed her hand.

"You will understand by the end of service."

Amara had sat up under the preaching and teaching of Pastor Rob since she was born. Asha would sometimes let Amara stay in adult services, but most of the time she went to Children's Church to learn the Word on a child's level. For the about the last year, Asha had slacked with her church attendance, but whenever Amara was with her grandmother they were at church bright and early.

They walked into the sanctuary and Amara was astonished by the sight before her. Everyone was dressed in some type of Army fatigue wear. When her grandmother had asked her back at the house did she have any, she thought it strange and said no. Amara had put on black fitted T-shirt and some black skinny jeans, but now she wished she would have put on the Army fatigue dress she had bought back in the summer.

The praise and worship team were singing a song about going to war. Everyone in the room was up on their feet singing with them. Amara saw clapping, stomping, some people jumping, some crying, and some down on their knees with their arms outstretched. Suddenly she did even need the Word for her to understand the theme.

Pastor Rob was getting his members ready to fight the enemy in a spiritual war. Amara recalled being taught how to war in the spirit, but it was still a concept she couldn't fully grasp. She hoped that after the revival she would have a better understanding.

Finally reaching a row that had empty seats, Amara went in first dancing her way to her seat. Another gift that she had was that she could hear a song one time and then be singing it like she wrote the song. She got to her seat and when into battle with the rest of the church. Amara felt someone tap her shoulder.

Turning around she started squealing when she saw her best friend Lysa standing next to her. Amara did not know what to say. She had lost contact with so many of her friends since the school year had started. Settling down, the girls took their seats and tried to gain control over their excitement.

Lysa had been her best friend at her old school. They had known each other since headstart. When Asha had married Dwayne and moved Amara away from her friends, Lysa's father had also remarried and moved away in the opposite direction. The girls never thought they would see each other again since they lived so far away. Amara knew now that she was truly meant to be in this service tonight.

Pastor Rob did an excellent job preaching the word from *Ephesians 6*, and then the praise team came back out with about 4 more songs. The whole time Amara kept get a feeling that something big was going to happen. Little did she know that what she was feeling was the Holy Spirit warning her.

Amara made Lysa promise to call her the next day before she left with her grandmother. Getting in the car, she braced herself for the millions of questions that she knew her grandmother was sure to have. Slowly Amara felt her eyes closing, but before they came to a complete close her grandmother started talking.

"So who was the little girl you were talking to? Did you even hear any of the messages being taught?"

"That was one of my old classmates and I heard everything that Pastor Rob said. The songs were catchy and I even downloaded a couple to my iTunes account."

"Oh that's nice, but I really don't like your tone of voice young lady!" "Oh Lord! Here we go again." Amara slapped her forehead and leaned against the door as far as possible from her grandmother. Alicia was noticing that Amara's attitude and behavior had been changing for the worse ever since she started going to that new school with those rich brats! She needed to do some serious praying. Asha was missing and Amara was acting like a completely different person. Not to mention that Alicia hadn't seen Dwayne in weeks. "Amara look I understand that there is a lot going on in your life right now, but you do not get to disrespect me. Do you want to talk about it?" "Ain't nothing to talk about," Amara said and then smacked her lips. "See that right there that is not allowed!" Alicia knew that now was the time to stop talking until they got home. If Amara had one more outburst or one more disrespectful moment, she was going to pull the car over and beat some sense into her. Finally they got home. Amara stomped in the house and up the stairs. Alicia was going to just let her go, but this weekend they would have a long talk.

CHAPTER EIGHT

Amara could feel that her weekend was going to be horrible! Saturday morning had started with Amara's grandmother waking her up by screaming at her about her behavior. Then telling her that she would be on punishment and stuck in her room until whenever her mother came back home. She would only be let out to go to school. Lysa had called and asked could she come over, but of course her grandmother said no.

After lying in her bed and sleeping most of the day, Amara had logged onto Instagram to see Taj in thousands of pictures with Sky at the party that she had invited her to. She was confused; Taj had asked her to go to the party and then disappeared. Her eyes started tearing up and she was trying to figure out what was happening.

Wiping her eyes and dialing Lace, Amara started feeling like she was about to have a mental breakdown. She hadn't even been in high school a whole month yet. She felt like she was hated already by most of the girls in the school. Her mother kept going on disappearing acts, only Lord knew where Dwayne was at, she barely saw her baby brother, and she missed all of her friends.

Amara pressed the end option, and debated on rather she should call Dontay. She hadn't talked to him since they exchanged numbers. Before she could dial his number though, her phone started ringing. It was a number she didn't recognize and she started not to answer it, but she swiped her finger right to answer.

"Hello."

"Hey Amara, this is Lace."

"Lace? Whose number is this?"

"I'm on my mother's phone because she took mine! I am so sick of her!"

"Lace calm down! First of all why did your mom take your phone and why do you keep making negative comments about her?"

Lace went on to fully explain the hatred that she had for her mother and begged Amara to ask her mother whenever she came home, could she come over there for a while. Amara promised that she would ask, but she really didn't see how that would work. Thinking about her mother must have made her mother think about her, her phone beeped alerting her to an incoming call.

"Mommy where are you and when are you coming back?"

Amara switched over and started talking without even telling Lace to hold. Her mother was really worrying her, she kept leaving without telling anybody where she was going. Amara wasn't sure if her mother even still had her job.

"No, the question is where are you?"

"Mommy, Delilah didn't show up or send anyone to get me, so grandma had to come pick me up yesterday."

"Amara what are you doing? Delilah called me and said she had no idea where you are at and you haven't been answering your phone!"

Oh boy, Amara thought. Delilah was back to her lying ways. Amara had called and heard Lace tell Delilah that she was at her grandmother's house yesterday afternoon before she got her phone took.

"Mommy, I did tell Delilah I was over here with grandma."

"Amara did I not tell you not to contact your grandmother?"

"Ma I am sick of being pulled in the middle of your mess! I called my grandmother because I did not have a ride! What would you rather I did, just sit outside the school until Monday morning?"

"Little girl I'm going to hang up this phone because I don't know who I am talking to. Goodbye!"

Asha disconnected the call before Amara could even respond. Amara threw the phone across the room. She had reached her breaking point and couldn't stop the tears from falling. She heard her phone ringing but she refused to get up and answer it. She sank down further in the pillow and pulled the cover over her head.

Alicia was trying to decide just how long she would let Amara stay in her room. Dwayne and her daughter Asha had both gone missing. Alicia could sense that her granddaughter was lost and confused. She was in a new environment practically all alone. However she still was not going to allow or tolerate disrespect.

As it started getting later and later, Alicia knew that Amara needed to come downstairs and eat. Plus if she slept all day, she would be up all night and would not want to go to church the next day.

"Amara!" she yelled up the stairs while walking into the kitchen to start a quick meal for the night.

Amara had been up for hours so she heard her grandmother calling her, but she wasn't going to go downstairs.

"Amara bring your behind out of that room, now!"

That was a sign that her grandmother was not going to take no for an answer. Slowly Amara got up out the bed. Truthfully she was starving but she was being stubborn. She was tired of all the adults in her life acting like kids. Her mother was gone, Dwayne had been missing for the last few weeks, her grandmother was getting on her nerves, and Delilah was always irritating.

After brushing her teeth and washing her face in the bathroom inside her bedroom, Amara finally went downstairs. Her grandmother had just started cooking but the kitchen already smelled good. Amara tried to still act like she wasn't hungry, but her stomach told on her.

"Is somebody hungry? Did I hear your stomach growling?"

Amara plopped down in the seat at the table and blew air out of her mouth.

"What is wrong with you young lady?"

"Why was you yelling like the food was already done?"

Amara was frustrated because she could still be lying in the bed. She only came downstairs because she wanted to eat.

Alicia slammed the spoon she was stirring the chili with on the stove and made it over to the table in what seemed like two steps.

"Amara, you better listen really closely and hear me loud and clear. I am tired of your smart mouth and disrespect. Do you understand me? Do not use that tone of voice with me anymore, or that smart mouth!"

"Grandma I'm just saying. I'm tired-"

"I don't care what you are JUST saying! Did you hear what I JUST said?"

Amara jumped up knocking the chair over and ran up the stairs, slamming the door when she got in the room.

Alicia was too shocked to move. This behavior was getting out of control and she wasn't sure how to handle her granddaughter at this very moment. So instead of marching up the stairs and knocking some sense into her, she walked over to the sink to rinse the spoon off so she could finish cooking. She stirred the chili a couple more times then started taking out the ingredients to make homemade biscuits.

***

THE SEARCH FOR AMARA

Amara felt guilty for acting disrespectful towards her grandmother. She was never the type of child to act like this towards any adults. Nobody understood what she was going through. Staring at her phone, Amara was trying to decide who to call. Somebody was going to give her some answers. Every time she had tried to call Dwayne, he didn't answer. She was going to make him answer tonight. To her surprise he answered on the second ring.

"Amara, hey sweetie!"

"Dwayne what is going on? Where are you?"

"Dammit! I knew she didn't tell you the truth!"

Amara was getting scared, she had never heard Dwayne curse and she was sure the 'she' that he was referring to was her mother.

"Listen Amara, where are you at right now?"

"I'm at my grandmother's, but you are worrying me."

"Are you going to be there tomorrow?"

"Yes. I don't know where my mother is. Grandma said I have to stay here until she comes back. I was over your sister's house at first."

"Ok. I promise I will be over there tomorrow to explain to you and your grandmother what is really going on."

Amara was really getting nervous now.

Dwayne talked to Amara for about another 45 minutes. Amara told him about the stuff that was going on in school. Dwayne gave her the same advice to watch out for Sky because she sounded like a bunch of trouble. After Dwayne promised one more time to come over tomorrow after church they ended the call.

Amara knew that she needed to go apologize to her grandmother. She felt horrible for lashing out at her grandmother when her grandmother was just worried about her. The revival had been awesome, but before they had even left Amara's grandmother had started being annoying. Her stomach was growling again and she knew that her grandmother wouldn't let her eat if she didn't apologize first.

She sent Dontay a text message and opened the Instagram app to see what her classmates were posting about. The first picture that popped up in her feed was a picture of Dontay and Courtney at the party. Taj was in the picture too, but Courtney's arms were hanging all over Dontay. Amara got pissed and wished she had gone on Instagram before she sent the text message.

Staring at the picture, Amara started questioning what could Tay possibly really see in her. Did he just look at her as a naive little girl? The new girl on the block so to speak. Was Taj setting her up again? Taj had been the one that swore Tay didn't talk to anyone at the school. Taj had also been the one though to invite Amara to the party and then left her after school.

Amara was so ready to go downstairs but she immediately got angry again. If her grandmother said something she didn't like she knew that would be disrespectful again. She was going to have to just suck up her feelings and go apologize cuz she had to get something to eat, and soon.

"Grandma!" Amara called out while walking down the stairs to the kitchen.

All of the lights were on downstairs, but her grandmother wasn't responding.

"Grandma!" Amara called out again a little louder when she reached the bottom of the stairs. Walking into the kitchen, the aroma of the chili made Amara's stomach growl loudly. She couldn't wait to get a huge bowl, along with a fresh biscuit that was cooling on top of the stove. Amara walked through the kitchen and continued the search for her grandmother. Walking past the den, she saw her grandfather watching one of his old western movies. He had been very distant for the past few months, so Amara decided not to disturb him. She had finally reached the back of the house and her grandmother was still nowhere to be seen, nor was she answering. "She left!" Amara's grandfather yelled out from the den. She couldn't believe that he had let her walk all through the house calling out for her grandmother to finally respond now that it was obvious that her grandmother had left. Amara was pissed all over again and stomped back upstairs. Anger had completely taken over and she didn't even want to eat anymore.

Chapter Nine

Sunday morning's service was always excellent, but Amara couldn't focus. The only thing on her mind was what news Dwayne was going to deliver. Amara never figured out where her grandmother had disappeared to yesterday either. Amara didn't know what was going on, but she was sick of all the secrecy.

"The Bible promises us that God is for us, He will never leave us or forsake us," Pastor Rob preached from the pulpit.

I sure don't feel God with me right now. Amara thought. Her phone had been vibrating for the past 30 minutes. She was so tempted to look at it, but she knew her grandmother would snatch it out of her hand and probably break it.

"I know someone out there is feeling like Pastor Rob doesn't know what he is talking about, but I promise no matter who has left you, God is still with you."

Amara's eyes shot up. She couldn't believe it! Looking over at her grandmother who was staring straight ahead smiling, Amara wasn't sure if she had really heard Pastor Rob say that or was it in her mind. Her mind began to wonder again. What if Dwayne was never coming back? What if her and Melissa were back together? Lace did say she heard Delilah talking to Melissa.

Finally Amara heard the praise team singing which meant service was about to be over. Pastor Rob asked everyone to stand so he could cover them with the benediction.

"Lord send your protection with everyone under the sound of my voice, in Jesus' name, amen! Have a blessed week and be a blessing to others."

Everyone started talking or making their exit. Amara hoped this was not one of those Sundays that her grandmother was going to go have 50 different conversations. She just wanted to hurry up home, so she could finally hear what Dwayne had to say. Pulling out her phone, she sent Dwayne a text letting him know she was on her way to the house before she checked all of her notifications.

Amara almost dropped the phone when she saw that she had four text messages from Tay. She also had one from Taj, two from Sky, one from an unknown number, and three from Lace. Panic washed over her, what was going on now. She didn't believe in coincidences, she felt drama lurking nearby.

"Grandma are you ready? Dwayne said he's on his way." Amara lied a little bit because she wanted her grandmother to hurry up and leave.

"Dwayne? On his way where?"

Oh shoot! Amara had completely forgot to tell her grandmother that she had talked to Dwayne and that he was coming over to tell them what was going on. She knew that her grandmother was about to go off, but maybe them still being in the church would save her; for the moment anyway.

"Amara when did you talk to Dwayne and when were you going to tell me he was coming?"

"Sorry grandma, I talked to Dwayne yesterday. When I came downstairs to tell you, you were gone. Where were you anyway?"

"That is none of your business. Let's go! Is he coming to the house?"

"Yes."

Alicia shook her head with aggravation. She had really wanted to have a meeting with Pastor Rob and Amara. Maybe it was a good thing that the meeting got postponed though, because Amara would need a lot of prayers very soon. They hurried out to the car, waving at members but not stopping to talk.

In what seemed like forever, they finally arrived at the house. Amara was not surprised that Dwayne was already there. She just hoped that her grandfather was in there being nice, and not in one of his moods. Amara stepped in the house and was relieved when she heard basketball stats being discussed and ESPN blaring from the flat screen that her grandmother had finally broken down and let her grandfather purchase for his den.

"Well hello there Dwayne," Alicia spoke up from behind Amara.

Amara was happy that Dwayne was here, but she was hesitating because she just knew that the dynamics of her family were about to change. Not for the better either.

"Hello Momma, how have you been? Hi Amara, are you going to speak?"

Amara stood still; she just wanted this moment to be over already.

"I've been great. I've been missing you and glad that you are back to talk to some sense into this child hopefully."

"Talk some sense into Amara? What's going on?"

"She's been acting like a spoiled damn brat!" Amara's grandfather answered, "And her mother has been acting like she don't have no damn kids! I don't know what's going with these women, my wife included."

"Excuse you!" Alicia said to her husband, Henry.

"Ok well if you all don't mind, I would like to sit down and speak to everyone at once. Amara and you both as well deserve some answers. Just be patient with me and understand that I can only talk from my perspective of this situation."

Henry and Alicia sat down, while Amara chose to keep standing. She was so sure that soon she would be walking out of the room. Dwayne's stalling told her that this meeting was going to be life-changing.

"Amara are you going to sit down?"

"No!"

"See Dwayne that type of behavior! You ask a simple question and she snaps your head off, that is not tolerated," Alicia spoke up before Dwayne could react.

"Amara," Dwayne spoke softly while walking towards her, "can you please come sit down with your grandparents?"

Amara stood with a look of defiance on her face. She was not going to sit down, and she wished that Dwayne would just start talking.

"Dwayne I do not want to sit down. Just get to it please, sheesh!"

"AMARA!" Alicia shouted and jumped up off the couch.

She reached the doorway where Amara was standing, snatched her by her arm and was ready to drag her across the room when Amara snatched her arm away.

"Get off of me, I AM NOT SITTING DOWN!"

"Now wait just a damn minute!" Henry said getting up now as well.

Dwayne couldn't believe what was taking place in front of him. He felt like Amara's behavior was partially his fault. He had to find a way to patch things up before he left. There was no way he could stay, and all though he felt horrible he and Asha were done.

"Ok please everyone let's just all calm down. Momma and Pops please calm down and we can just let Amara stand up.

Amara honey, I understand your frustration and anger, but you cannot disrespect your grandparents. You owe them an apology."

"Sorry. Now can you get this over with? PLEASE!"

Alicia looked over at Dwayne and had to bite the inside of her cheek. He finally started talking and creating a clear picture of what was going on without throwing Asha under the bus. The truth was that the couple had not been happy since the wedding. They had several arguments, almost daily but the final straw was finding out that Asha was cheating this time around.

Dwayne knew that he had done his wrong in the past and he was not trying to justify his actions, but he had a little bit of a reason behind his. To his knowledge, Asha had been cheating for some time and she had admitted that she wasn't sure if DJ was his child. They agreed to stay apart until the results came in, because Dwayne couldn't look at her without getting full of rage.

Amara and her grandparents just stared in shock. Amara decided that now would be a good time to sit down, especially since her tears were racing down her face were clouding her sight. She knew it was going to be bad, but not this bad. She didn't know what she was going to do, and she was worried thinking about if her mother was going to come back. Delilah hadn't called her grandmother back yet, and Amara needed her little brother in her presence. "So Dwayne what is the plan? Are you and Asha going to go to counseling or are you finished and going to get a divorce?" "Pops this is why I really wished that Asha would have talked to you all instead of running away. I had tried as hard as I could to get her to bring everyone together but she kept refusing and that is why I left. I filed divorce papers as soon she admitted to me the truth." "NOOOOOOOOOOOO!" Amara cried out and ran upstairs. Alicia and Henry sat in silence. They couldn't believe that their daughter would get herself caught up like this. Alicia was crying and apologized to Dwayne. She told him that he had some tough choices to make, because Amara really looked at him as a father figure. Dwayne was glad that the burden was lifted off of his shoulders. He promised that he would call Amara later and check on her. He thought it was best to leave her alone for now.

CHAPTER TEN

Amara cried all night. She was so mad at her mother and she had no one she could talk to since Lace was on punishment. Her alarm went off alerting her it was time to get up and get ready for school. She was considering asking her grandmother could she stay home, but felt like going to school may be the distraction she needed.

"Amara," her grandmother called as she opened the door.

"Come in grandma."

Alicia entered into the room not sure what to expect. She felt bad for being so hard on her granddaughter with everything that had been going on. Amara had always had a special gift of knowing things before they happened.

"Did you know, I mean did you see this coming?"

"Grandma I knew it was going to be bad, but not this bad. I thought that Dwayne had messed up not mommy. Especially since Lace told me that Melissa was back in the picture."

"Wow, this is a lot. Do you want to stay home from school?"

"I thought about it, but I think I will enjoy the distraction of classes."

"Ok well I will go make you a healthy breakfast. Blueberry pancakes?"

"Yummy, thanks grandma!" Amara said while getting up to kiss her grandmother on the cheek.

Alicia got up to go back downstairs, closing the door behind her. Amara really did want to go to school but she was not okay. She felt like God had let her down again. First her daddy, now her mother. She would probably never have a genuine relationship with Dwayne now because she would hardly ever see him.

What's the point of doing right, Amara thought. She had tried all of her life to be a good girl, but it wasn't enough. She was going to enjoy her life now and have fun to keep her mind off of the crazy life she was now being forced to live. Getting her things together to go take a shower, she remembered that she never checked her text messages yesterday.

Opening Tay's first, she couldn't do nothing but laugh. The first message told her not to believe everything she saw on the gram (Instagram), the other ones were him asking her why wasn't she responding to him. The three from Lace were telling her that she was sneaking on her phone and she would call her as soon as she got her phone back, but she had overheard her mother telling Melissa that Dwayne was getting a divorce.

Taj had apologized; her mother had picked her up early and upset so she couldn't wait for her. Her phone had died so she couldn't text. Amara laughed again because Taj must have thought she was stupid or something. That was a good explanation but why didn't she text Friday night or even Saturday?

Sky had just wanted to know if she was still going to help her with the assignment for class. The unknown number was quickly recognized when she read the message. It was Courtney again, telling her to check out the pictures of proof and issuing another 'warning'.

Amara shook her head and continued her morning hygiene ritual. She prayed that Courtney stayed out of her way. They were about to meet a new Amara. No more good girl. She needed lots of excitement.

Putting the phone on the dresser, she went to take her shower. When she got out 15 minutes later, her head was full of ideas. She put her hair up in high ponytail and looked through the drawers in the bathroom. She remembered her grandmother had given her some old makeup to play with but she was going to wear it today. It wasn't much, just some mascara and lipstick.

Once she was satisfied with the look, she moved onto to her uniform next. She usually wore undershirt under her school shirt but today she was going to just wear her bra with the top button undone. Even though she was young she was blessed at the top thanks to her mother and grandmother. Amara wasn't completely crazy though, she knew she couldn't unbutton that top button until she got to school. Her grandmother would kill her. She sprayed herself down with some *Sheer Love* from *Victoria's Secret*.

Next she put some leggings on up under her school pants, to make the pants fit tighter. She had saw Sky do this at school one day. At the time she thought it was stupid, but now the idea came in handy. Amara had a point to prove. She didn't even like Dontay anymore because he was a liar, but she wasn't going to let Courtney think she could have him either.

The devil was putting all types of poison in Amara's head and sadly she didn't even understand the war that was going on. Even though she had just went to a revival on spiritual warfare. But this was how the enemy worked and Amara was about to enter her first personal spiritual battle.

She was satisfied with her look for the time being until she got to school, so she gathered her things and made her way downstairs. As soon as she entered the kitchen her grandmother started praying out loud without even turning around. When Alicia turned around she received the shock of her life. Amara looked like she was almost sixteen years old or older.

"Lord please be with our family in this time of the need. We need you right now."

Amara sat at the table and dug right into her food without even blessing it.

"Amara honey don't let your circumstances change you. Stay true to who you are."

Alicia decided that was all she was going to say and walked out the kitchen before Amara saw the tears forming in her eyes. The storm was brewing and Alicia knew it would get worse before it got better. Nobody could have prepared her just how bad it would get though.

***

"Dannnnng Amara, shorty where you been hiding all that body?"

The boys were going crazy, exactly the reaction Amara was looking for. She was only looking for it from one boy in particular though, and she hadn't seen him yet. She noticed Sky, Courtney, and Taj all standing together by the door. They were trying to figure out who had the guys are riled up. Sky instantly got upset when she saw Amara. Taj and Courtney didn't recognize her, and Taj felt a little threatened.

"Amara!" Sky called out.

"AMARA!" Taj and Courtney said in unison.

"Hey y'all how was the party? You guys looked like y'all were having fun!"

Taj and Courtney were speechless. Courtney knew that if she ever even had a chance with Dontay, her chances were definitely gone now.

"Girl did somebody pop your cherry or something?" Sky asked with laughter in her voice.

"Girl please! You tried it! I'm just trying something new. I mean we are in high school right?"

"Yeah, you're right."

Sky and Amara continued their conversation, while Taj and Courtney couldn't figure out what to say.

Dontay walked up and grabbed Amara from behind while whispering in her ear.

"Oh so you're just going to keep ignoring me?"

Amara was in trouble, she thought she would be able to pull this off but immediately her inexperience kicked in.

"Eww get off of me!" she squealed while wiggling out of his grasp.

Courtney just looked and laughed. She knew that Amara had no clue what to do with Dontay. If that was her in his arms, she would have eaten him up. Dontay looked embarrassed but he quickly regained his cool.

"Amara don't act like that. Come here baby. I said I was sorry."

Dontay was willing to put on a show even if meant causing him embarrassment. He saw something in Amara that he knew he had to have, and it was not just about sex. Courtney could not believe that he was out here begging for Amara's attention. Sky couldn't take it and had to put the attention back on her.

"Oh so that's why you couldn't help me Amara, you were laid up with Dontay? Ok girl I ain't even mad at you no more."

Amara face got red hot; she could not believe that Sky was trying to put her out there like that. Before she could respond though, Dontay spoke up.

"Sky don't do that. I thought you were her friend. Why would you try to put our business out there? Especially when it's not even true?"

THE SEARCH FOR AMARA

A smile spread across Amara's face and the same time a frown graced Sky's face. Nothing else could be said because the warning bell alerted them that it was time to get into the building and head to first hour class. Dontay grabbed Amara's hand and they entered into the building together. Amara felt like a princess, but she tried not to smile because she really was mad at Dontay.

She understood why girls went so crazy over boys, they were confusing. Amara had seen the pictures for herself on Instagram, but Dontay had told her not to believe everything she saw. Judging by what he had just done, she felt like she had no need to worry about Courtney but at the same time she was still confused.

Amara had never really liked a boy, so she wasn't sure how she was supposed to feel. Sometimes she really like Dontay and sometimes she like him the same as any other friend.

"Amara I will be here at the end of the period to walk you to your next class. You look really pretty today, but don't lower yourself to these girls' standards. You feel me?" "Yeah, thanks Tay." Now Amara really felt stupid. She walked in the class and immediately asked for a hall pass to go to the bathroom. Once there she washed her face and took her ponytail out, she went in one of the stalls and took her leggings off. She folded them up and put them in her book bag. She was glad that she had an extra shirt in her bag, and she put it on under her school shirt. Walking out of the stall, she stared at herself in the mirror. *Girl what are you doing?* Amara questioned. She had never felt the need to be someone she wasn't, and why did she let Courtney take her to this point if she didn't even like Dontay? Little did she know that this was just the beginning.

CHAPTER ELEVEN

Things had quieted down a little bit. DJ was home with Amara at their grandparents' house. Nobody had heard Asha's voice but she was texting Amara daily to check on them. Lace was finally off of punishment and she was coming over this weekend since they didn't have school Monday. Alicia had also agreed to let Lysa come over. Asha was looking forward to a weekend with like-minded people. Even though Lace was younger she would still fit in, because they would be talking about celebrities and normal stuff. Not about the latest drama and boyfriends, or so Asha had thought.

Friday had finally come on the heels of a lot of drama at school all week. Sky was doing her best to make Courtney mad, but she didn't realize that she was making Amara look bad. Even though Amara just wanted to ignore her, Dontay was furious. Amara kept telling Sky that she didn't need her help because she was not worried about Courtney. Taj was caught in the middle.

Taj really liked Amara, and she saw that Amara was a good friend. She had felt bad about bailing out at the last minute on Amara. Courtney had flipped out and had a fit when she told her that she had invited Amara, so instead of being caught in the middle she had just called her driver and dipped out early.

Right before lunch Dontay had embarrassed Amara but also made her feel things she had never felt before when he pushed her up against her locker and kissed her. He held her head and place and pushed his tongue in her mouth. At first she didn't know what to do but after a few seconds it came like second nature. She was breathless and a little sad when he pulled away. He smiled and walked away leaving her at the locker.

That kiss had been the talk of the rest of the day and Amara felt important. She didn't even realize that she was creating enemies left and right. Who was this new brilliant freshman that had come in and swept the junior that girls had been trying to get with for years off of his feet. Almost every girl in the school was envious of Amara and some had started plotting against her, especially Courtney.

At the end of the day, Amara was walking out to meet her grandmother while secretly wondering where Tay was at. When she reached the door to go outside, it was a group of girls blocking her exit. She made sure her face didn't change. She was not scared, but she would be lying if she said she wasn't a little bit intimidated. Amara decided she wouldn't say anything she would just push past them.

"Excuse you bitch!" One of the girls said while pushing Amara into another girl.

Amara tried to keep her balance and not fall into the other girl, but it was too late. Before she could catch herself the girl shoved her hard back the other way which caused her to fall into the wall. The push was hard and knocked a lot of air out of her lungs.

She was trying to get herself together because she felt a little dizzy, when one of the girls behind her grabbed her hair pulling her backwards. Once she finally hit the floor, they all started kicking her. One of the girls was about to stomp on her face when she heard Dontay yelling and heard the girls screaming and running away.

"Amara what happened?"

Amara was crying so hard she couldn't even answer. Although she didn't even know what had happened anyway. She had never been in a fight in her whole life, and she couldn't figure out why the girls would jump her. Looking down she was glad that had put an undershirt on earlier in the day, because the girls had ripped her school shirt when they were pushing her back and forth.

She finally got up off the floor and snatched her stuff away from Dontay running out the doors. Amara was glad it was Friday, and there was no school on Monday. Hopefully by Tuesday this moment would be forgotten. She didn't need answers; she knew that the girls had jumped on her because of Dontay. However what she didn't know was that Sky had created a fake Facebook page in her name and was making crazy statuses.

When she reached her grandmother's car, she had forgotten that quick that she looked a mess.

"Amara what the heck happened to you? Were you fighting?"

"No"

"Then why do you look like that? Why are your clothes all tore up and your hair all over your head?"

"Grandma, I'm fine! Can we please just go get Lace and go home?" Amara turned and looked at her grandma. Alicia could see the hurt and confusion in Amara's eyes and for that reason she left it alone, put the car in drive, and pulled out into traffic.

Amara closed her eyes and tried to remember if she knew or recognized any of the girls that were part of the senseless act. She thought that the girls must be seniors because she couldn't remember ever seeing any of them. The senior class had all of their classes on the third floor, so the under classmen didn't see them often. They even had their own lunch period.

"Amara if somebody jumped on you, they need to suffer the consequences."

"Grandma really we were just playing and I fell too hard. Seriously I am ok."

Alicia knew that Amara was not telling the truth, but she knew when the other girls came over tonight they would talk about what really happened and hopefully she would be able to hear the truth then.

Amara's phone started chiming; she only checked it because it could have been Lysa or Lace. She had put the text message notifications on default, so everyone had the same. She got tired of trying to remember who had which ringtone. It was Taj asking what happened and was she ok. Amara text back and told her she still didn't know what happen but she was ok.

Lace called to make sure Amara was still coming to pick her up. They talked a few more minutes and then Amara ended the call. She was glad that her girls were coming over, but she couldn't wait to get in her bed. Her body was getting sore. Amara still couldn't process that she had got jumped. Especially by some girls she didn't even know.

Amara found it very interesting that neither Sky nor Dontay had sent a message to see if she was ok. This was the final straw. Courtney she could handle, but Amara was not going to get jumped on over Dontay. These jealous girls could have him. Out of nowhere she just broke down in gut wrenching sobs. Her grandmother quickly pulled into a convenience store parking lot.

"Amara baby, please talk to me. What is going on?"

Alicia had a strong feeling this story had something to do with a boy. Immediately all types of thoughts started going through her head. The way Amara had dressed this morning to leave the house, had Alicia praying all day. She especially prayed that Amara was not out here having sex with these little wild boys.

"Grandma these girls jumped me today after school when I was on my way out to the car!" Amara finally managed to get out between all of her sobs.

"What did they jump on you for? I know you don't bother nobody! Was it that damn Sky girl?"

That was a good question, but one that Amara could not answer. She really had no idea why the girls had jumped on her. She wouldn't know probably until Tuesday, if she ever found out.

"Grandma truthfully I do not know."

Amara's phone started ringing with the ringtone that she had selected for Dontay. It sounded like police sirens, a warning to remind her that he was dangerous.

"Hello."

"Oh my goodness Amara, are you ok?"

"Yeah."

"Look I know that you are upset. The reason it took so long for me to call you, is because I was trying to figure out why the hell those girls jumped on you. Where are you at?"

"I'm in the car with my grandma, on my way home." "Okay, good! Do you think she would let me come over to talk to you?" Amara didn't realize that her phone volume was so loud. "Is that the nice young man that I met the other day?" "Yes" "Tell him sure he can come over, I will order pizza and wings for everybody." "Well since she heard you, I am quite sure you heard her. I will see you in a little bit." Amara gave Dontay the address before hanging up. She hoped since Lace and Lysa would be there, her grandma would let them all go up to her room. She really needed to lie down. She squeezed Amara's hand, gave her big smile, and pulled out the parking lot to go pick up Lace.

CHAPTER TWELVE

As soon as Amara got to her room, she took two Tylenol and went to go to take a hot shower. She had never felt like pain in her body like this before. Lace really had no idea what to say. She was still waiting for Amara to tell her what happened. Lace could tell that Amara was in pain but she didn't know if it was physical or emotional pain.

Lace sat down on the floor and was responding to a group chat she was in on Kik. This generation was very well advance in the things that they knew about life, and technology was not helping them either by allowing them access to many different things. Lace was only eleven years old but the group she was in was discussing one of her friends who had recently had sex.

Lace was so busy reading and typing that she barely heard Amara come back in the room. Amara still had her towel wrapped around her as she pulled her hair out of the ponytail on top of her head. Pulling out her dresser drawers she grabbed a clean pair of blue & gray pajamas. Opening another drawer she pulled out some socks. She opened the final drawer, grabbed some underwear, and went back into the bathroom to get dressed.

When Amara came back into the room, Lace was on her laptop scrolling through Facebook.

"Why are you being nosey?"

"You know my mother won't let me have a Facebook page, Every time I try to sneak, she finds out about it and shuts it down. I don't even understand the big deal. Everyone is on Instagram, Kik or Snapchat now anyway."

"Yeah you're right. I don't really be on any social media much, they are all overrated, and people always creating some type of drama."

"Right so are you ready to tell me what happened?"

Amara got quiet and just stared across the room for a minute. She really didn't want to keep talking about this.

"Lace I will tell you when everyone gets here. I don't want to keep telling the same story. I'm going to lie down until Lysa and Tay get here."

With that being said Amara went and laid across her bed pulling her Mickey Mouse over her feet and legs. Lace got up from the desk and went to lie down next to Amara. She didn't know what was going on, but she felt like her big cousin needed her. She wanted to tell her what she had heard her mother telling Melissa, but she knew was not a good time.

Lace closed her eyes and before long she was sound asleep right alongside Amara. Lace didn't know how long she had been sleep, but she heard Grandma Alicia calling them to come downstairs. Lace shook Amara to wake her up.

"OOOOOUUUCCCHHHH!!!"

Lace almost fell off the bed she jumped back so quickly. Amara had scared the life out of her.

"I am so sorry Amara. Are you okay?"

Lace wanted to burst out in tears; she had totally forgotten that Amara was in pain. She stared at Amara whose body was shaking. Lace felt horrible.

"Amara are you ok?"

Amara couldn't hold it in anymore she rolled over cracking up laughing.

"That is not funny Amara; I thought I had hurt you!"

Lace was on the verge of tears, Amara was in so much pain earlier. How could she forget that quickly?

"I'm sorry Lace. I feel so much better now. What were you shaking me for anyways?"

"AMARA come downstairs!"

"That's why I was shaking you."

The girls got up and started making their way downstairs. When they get to the bottom of the stairs they heard multiple voices coming from the kitchen. Amara knew for sure that the one voice she was hearing was Dontay's, but she could identify the other male voice.

When the girls entered the kitchen, they were very shocked and a little nervous to see a cop standing in the doorway. Alicia spoke up first.

"Amara honey, this is Officer Ryan. Dontay called him to come over. Sit down so we can fill you in on what is going on."

Amara tried to move but her feet felt like they were glued to the floor. The thought of *What could possibly be this serious?* raced through her mind. Lace nudged her a little trying to get her to go and sit down. Dontay came over and grabbed Amara's hand.

"Amara this is going to sound really crazy so please come and sit down."

Alicia looked in awe. She knew that this young man was four year older than her granddaughter, but she could see and feel the genuine compassion that he held for Amara. It made Alicia think back to when she and Henry were younger. She was so happy because she didn't think that there were any teens like that around anymore.

The church ladies would always be gossiping about which young girl was having sex, on birth control, or sadly had contracted a STD. Alicia wanted to believe that her precious Amara was still a virgin, but one could never be 100% certain. Especially with Asha running around and disappearing all the time lately.

Amara finally walked over the counter and sat on the edge of one of stools. Lace came and stood next to her, but before Officer Ryan could start talking, the doorbell rang. Alicia called out and asked Henry to get the door.

"It's probably Lysa," Amara said quietly.

"Well let's get started," Officer Ryan spoke up, "Amara did you recognize any of the girls?"

"No."

"Well you shouldn't have, they don't go to your school. We are still trying to figure out how they got in the building."

"Amara, how are you feeling?" Dontay asked.

"I feel better now since I took some Tylenol and had a quick nap."

"Amara someone created a fake Facebook page in your name with a lot of your pictures to help make it look legit. Also I don't know who was out there but someone videotaped the fight and it is already all over social media."

Amara was furious, "it was not a fight! Those girls jumped me!" Amara burst out in tears again for the second time in hours.

Officer Ryan was like most men, and hated to see women cry. Dontay and Lace were trying to provide Amara with comfort. Alicia left out to see what was taking Henry so long at the door. She had another surprise waiting for her.

Henry turned around when he heard Alicia walk into the living room.

"These young ladies are looking for Amara."

"Hi Lysa. How are you?"

"I'm good Mrs. Alicia."

"Hello young lady what is your name?" Alicia asked Taj.

"Hi ma'am my name is Taj."

"Hi, Taj. What is your full name and what can I help you with?

"My name is Tajsa. It means born into royalty."

Something about the look on Alicia and Henry's faces made Taj feel like she had to explain why her parents have given her such a name.

"That's beautiful, but what can I help you with?

"I'm sorry. I go to school with Amara and I was coming to check on her."

"Is that right? How did you know where to come? Amara doesn't live here."

Taj immediately got nervous; she had people do her some favors to find Amara, because she would not be able to wait until Tuesday to see if Amara was ok. Alicia was staring at her and Taj could tell that she was waiting for an answer. Alicia's glare and presence told Taj that lying would not be a good idea.

"I was really worried about my friend, so I had the lady in the office to get me the emergency contact information out of her file. Please don't be mad at the school, I am so sorry."

Alicia invited both young ladies in the house and they made their way back to the kitchen. Once everyone was gathered in the kitchen, Dontay continued explaining everything that he knew along with somethings he assumed were going on. When he finished talking, Officer Ryan took over the conversation.

The video was being investigated, and as soon as the girls were identified they would be facing criminal charges. Officer Ryan assured Amara that he would make sure the girls were charged with the most serious offense. He also told everyone that he would be going to pay Sky a visit. He and Dontay were almost certain without a doubt that she was behind the fake Facebook page.

Officer Ryan finished up guaranteeing that he would not rest until those girls were arrested. He told Amara to get some rest, and enjoy her three day weekend. He turned to leave out the kitchen, and Alicia informed him that she would walk him to the door.

Dontay said that he had some things to take care of. He had really just came over to make sure for himself that Amara was ok, and to bring Officer Ryan to talk to her. Alicia walked back in the kitchen carrying boxes of pizza, just as Dontay was leaving out with Amara following behind him.

"Oh no, you can't leave without eating," Alicia told Dontay blocking his exit.

"Thank you ma'am, but I am going to have turn down your offer, I have some important things to take care of at home."

"Yeah grandma, Dontay just came over to check on me. He was just telling us how he had to finish up some things at home."

"Well, ok. At least let me wrap up some pizza for you to take with you. Wait how are you getting home? I thought you came with Officer Ryan."

"That's easy. I live around the corner!"

"What?" Amara exclaimed.

She couldn't believe that he lived around the corner from her grandmother.

"So why do you go to Westbourne Academy?"

"My mom didn't want to move out of the neighborhood, but my dad didn't want me in this school system. Said he didn't want to worry about his son going to school with some of the same people he had arrested in the past."

"Wait a minute; Officer Ryan is your father?"

"That would be correct."

"Wow you are just full of surprises today," Alicia said while placing the pizza wrapped in foil into his hands.

Amara continued walking Dontay to the door in shock. She could not believe that as many times as she came over her grandma's and played in the neighborhood, she had never laid eyes on Dontay. Truthfully though, she probably wouldn't have noticed Dontay at school either. Even if she did, she wouldn't have spoken to him if he didn't speak to her first.

The girls went one by one to the small bathroom off the kitchen to wash their hands, and then came back to the counter to devour pizza and make small talk. Knowing that Alicia wasn't too far away, they kept their conversation very basic. Amara whispered they would talk more when they made it upstairs.

Amara welcome the small talk though, because she was not ready to talk about what was going on. It would be hard for to put into words what she didn't really understand yet herself. She knew Lace would want to talk about Dwayne and Melissa; another topic that she did not want to discuss, and certainly not in front of Lysa. Amara hated making people feel uncomfortable.

"Do you want the last slice?" Lysa asked Amara, but secretly she was hoping Amara turned it down.

"No I am stuffed go ahead."

Lace just looked in disbelief, she remembered Lysa a little bit, but she did not like her too much.

"No I don't want it either. Thanks for asking."

Lysa stopped mid chew and glared at Lace.

"Well you sat there for so long without even looking. I assumed you were finished eating." "Yep, you know what they say about assuming?' "Lace that is not necessary." Amara knew where Lace was trying to take the conversation so she hurried to put an end to it. Amara got up and started cleaning up the kitchen so the girls could go upstairs. The atmosphere started feeling very awkward. Amara didn't want something out of nothing, but she sensed that there was some heavy animosity between Lace and Lysa. She decided that would be addressed and handled as soon as they got in the room. Taking a final look around the kitchen, satisfied that everything was clean, Amara turned off the lights and prepared the girls to go upstairs.

CHAPTER THIRTEEN

The girls had settled their differences that night for the sake of coming together for one another. Taj turned out to be a God send to Amara. A lot that they had discussed that night brought them closer together. It was comforting to know that no one was going through things by themselves.

Asha was still texting to check on Amara, but had not been home. Lace was still not sure what was going on with Delilah. Lysa had dropped on bomb when she told everyone that her parents were getting a divorce after being married for 35 years. Taj told the girls that she was going through the norm with her parents, which was her parents being too caught up in themselves to know what was going on with her.

An unbreakable bond was formed that night months ago, and now that Christmas break was right around the corner, the girls were trying to decide what they were going to do for two weeks. Dontay had been another constant in Amara's life, but right now they had decided to just remain close friends. Sky had seemed to have disappeared off the face of the earth and the girls that had jumped on Amara had been arrested and were now on probation. All had been quiet and calm in Amara's life, but there always seemed to be an unsettling calm before a huge storm.

"Hey girl what you doing?" Taj asked Amara when she answered the phone.

"Staring in my closet trying to figure out what to wear to the winter formal."

"What? You're not buying a new dress?"

"Taj, you know I can't just up on go buy a dress. I still have no idea where my mother is, so I try not to use the credit card."

"You know if you want a dress, I got you covered."

"Taj now you know--"

"Amara cut it out; anyway I called you to tell you some hot juicy gossip I got a hold to!"

Taj had heard from someone that Sky had moved, because she was in foster care and when she had got in trouble for the Facebook incident, the provider asked for her to be removed from the home. Amara felt a little bad. She had no idea that Sky was in foster care. How could her caretakers afford to send her to Westbourne, then Amara remembered that Sky had been in attendance due to a scholarship.

Taj suggested that they go to the mall and look for dresses. Amara told her that she had to ask her grandma and she would call back shortly. Going to seek approval, Amara was greeted by DJ in the hallway. Amara absolutely loved and adored her baby brother. She was wondering why he was sitting in the hallway by himself.

Upon further examination downstairs, Amara found both of her grandparents sleep in their room. She didn't want to disturb them, but she also didn't want to stay in the house.

"Grandma...grandma...grandm--"

"Stop calling her, what do you want?" her grandfather interjected.

"Can I go with Taj to the mall? I will take DJ."

"Sure. Just make sure everything is cleaned and put away in their proper places."

Amara switched DJ to the other hip and walked out of the room wanting to run. She knew she was pushing her limits, getting permission from her grandfather when her grandmother was more than likely to have told her no.

Leaving out the room, she rushed up to her room to call Taj so she could be on her way. It seemed like time was standing still. She didn't want to risk her grandmother waking up and changing her plans.

Thirty minutes later, hearing her grandfather snoring all the way upstairs, Amara tiptoed downstairs with a sleeping DJ, and out the door. Taj's driver pulled up at the same time Amara pulled the door closed quietly behind her. Amara wasn't even thinking about the fact that DJ would need a car seat, so she just put him between her and Taj and prayed for the best. She could not believe that in a way, she had just snuck out of the house.

They arrived at the mall and DJ was still asleep. Amara was starting to realize this might have been a horrible idea. DJ was too heavy to be carrying around the mall. They went to the security booth and asked did the mall have strollers that they could rent.

Thank goodness they did. She laid DJ down in the stroller and the girls got started on their journey.

Taj led them into a small store that had beautiful gowns that looked like the expensive evening dresses that Amara was only used to seeing on television. Amara was in awe as she walked around the store. Walking to the back of the store, she saw some dresses that looked more reasonably priced.

"Taj come look at these back here," Amara mentioned over her shoulder.

Taj walked over with another gown in her hand. It was a red floor length dress with a split up one side. It looked pretty boring to Amara but she would keep her thoughts to herself, because obviously Taj liked it. To her surprise though Taj had picked it out for her.

"Amara you would look fabulous in this, you should try it on."

"Oh no, I don't want anything that expensive for basically a one-time thing. Where else could I possibly wear this to?"

"Honey you can just add it to your wardrobe, go try it on. You will love it once you see yourself in it."

Amara reluctantly took the dress and headed to the dressing room. She hurriedly put the dress on so she could get this over with, without hurting Taj's feelings. This dress was simply just not her style. Once she had it on, she walked out the dressing room to show Taj. She looked around and didn't see Taj at first but there was another group of her girls standing by a rack of dresses.

"Hahaha, look at her in that dress! Doesn't she know that is not one size fits all? Why would she squeeze her fat ass in that little dress?"

Amara made eye contact with one of the girls who look ashamed but didn't open her mouth. Tears threatened to fall from Amara's eyes as she turned around and hurried back into the dressing room. She took the dress off, threw it on the floor, put her clothes back on, and stomped back into the store looking for Taj.

"Taj this wasn't a good idea, I'm ready to go."

"Wait what happened? You didn't like the dress?"

"Taj I'm just ready to go home."

"Ok Amara, sheesh let's go."

Taj was confused, she didn't know what had just happened but they had just got there and now Amara had an attitude. She would just have her driver take Amara back home, she wasn't leaving.

"Wow ok. I don't know what's going on. I'm not ready to leave, but my driver will take you."

"Yeah whatever. I'm going to the food court. Can you just have him meet me?"

Amara walked away before Taj could even respond. She made her way back out into the mall and over to the food court. The smell of the food was making her sick to her stomach. She couldn't believe that the girl had called her fat. The more and more she thought about, was she fat? Amara was much bigger than everyone else she knew. She never considered herself fat, her grandmother always just referred to her as healthy.

She thought back to when she altered her look that day, and how all the boys were going crazy. Hadn't they liked it or did they consider her fat too? She held DJ closer to her to comfort herself while she was waiting for the car to pull up. The longer she sat there, the more she heard the voices in her head telling her that she was fat. When the driver pulled up, Amara face was soaked with tears running down her face. This was another attack in her battle.

DJ had woken up and was talking Amara's ear off but she couldn't focus to pretend like she understood his baby talk. The ride that seemed like it was taking forever finally came to an end when the driver pulled in her grandmother's driveway. Amara grabbed DJ and got out the car without saying goodbye.

Walking into the house she was greeted by her grandmother yelling at her. "Amara where in the world where you? When did you start leaving without permission?" "I did have permission," Amara said leaving DJ in the living room and stomping up the stairs. "Lord please help me not hurt this girl!" Alicia prayed out loud. Later on that night, Alicia had gone to get Amara for dinner. Alicia didn't know how much of this teenage attitude she could take or how much longer. She left Amara in her room to sulk, and went downstairs to get in contact with Asha. It was time for her to come home and get her house in order. Asha was not answering, so Alicia went into her room and began to pray.

CHAPTER FOURTEEN

That incident at the mall had been the trigger that sent Amara into a deep depression and an obsession in her weight. She didn't go to the winter formal and faked being sick so that she didn't have to be around the girls over the Christmas break. When it was time to go back to school, Amara had lost about five pounds because wasn't eating. She would make food and throw it away so that her grandmother wouldn't become suspicious.

She liked the changes in her clothes but she wasn't happy. The five pounds was not nearly enough. Amara wore a size ten in pants and a medium in shirts, but after that girl at the mall she was determined to go down to a size four.

The second week back in school after the Christmas break, Taj told her about another party she wouldn't want to miss. Amara and her grandmother hadn't been getting along so she knew she probably was not going to be able to go.

"You don't think she would let you spend the night?" Taj asked.

"I doubt it. We haven't been seeing eye to eye on anything. I really wish my mother would just come back home."

"Dang Amara, I don't know which is worse. Having parents that are physically or mentally missing."

"Wow! Taj that is deep. Hey you want to come over here this weekend?"

"Will your grandma let me?"

"Of course! She loves you, and she will love the idea that I'm in the house."

"Yeah that would probably be more fun than that party anyway."

"Oh we are going to that party, I have an idea."

Taj didn't know what Amara had planned. She was just happy to see her friend out of her slump. Something had happened in the mall Taj knew for sure, she just didn't know what and Amara refused to talk about it.

The girls finished up their conversation; they both had a ton of homework to do. When Amara ended the call on her end, she got up and walked over to the mirror. Staring at herself she noticed some changes, but she turned to the side and held in her stomach. *Ten more pounds*, Amara thought. The sad thing was Amara was perfectly fine and healthy. She didn't even have a stomach.

Walking over to her computer, she sat down and went online. She Googled weight loss and diet pills. She had seen a commercial the other day that guaranteed results in just two days but she couldn't remember the name of the company. At the time she couldn't write down the information because she watching a show with her grandmother.

There were so many different pills available and all of them offered amazingly quick results. Amara just settled on the ones that were the least expensive. Since the credit card was in her mother's name, she could easily order the pills. Now the only problem was where she could get the pills sent to. Dontay came to mind and she decided to give him a call.

"Hey I thought you forgot I was alive!"

"Sorry Dontay, I just been going through a lot."

"I know, that is why I am here Amara, remember?"

"Yeah I know Dontay, but there are some things I just don't feel comfortable talking to you about. Anyway I need a favor."

"Wow, you don't call me until you need something."

"Dontay it is not even like that. I don't need you to do anything; I just need to send a package to your address."

"A package? What?"

Amara had to think quickly. She couldn't tell Dontay what she was ordering, she knew he would not agree and try to talk her out of it.

"I'm ordering my grandmother a gift and I want it to be a surprise."

"Oh ok, I will do it for your grandma."

"Whatever Dontay, what is your address?"

Dontay gave her the information and Amara ended the call with a promise to call him back in a couple of hours. She jumped up from the desk so excited that she was able to get the pills. The ten pounds she wanted to lose would be gone in a matter of days as soon as she got her hands on the pills.

The weekend was here and Alicia had agreed to let Taj spend the night. The girls were in Amara's room Friday night playing with DJ and watching *Bring It*! It was a hit show with teenage girls and even some parents nationwide about dancing teenage girls. Amara wanted to be a cheerleader, but Westbourne didn't have a cheerleading team. The really didn't have an athletic department at all.

After all who had time for sports? They were worried about the latest fashions, the newest technology, and the hottest parties. Speaking of which Taj hadn't mentioned the party again, so Amara brought it up.

"Is the party still tomorrow?"

Taj stopped playing with DJ and looked at her.

"Why? What are you thinking?"

"I'm thinking that I want to go!"

"How?"

"Easy! On Saturday's this house shuts down early. Everyone will be sleep and we can sneak out!"

"Amara are you serious?"

"YES!"

"Ok bad ass, how are we going to get there?"

"Where is the party at?"

"All the way on the other side of town."

"Ok we can just call a cab."

"I can't believe that you are really considering this."

"Why not? I am tired of being the only one obeying rules around here."

"Why didn't you tell me your plan before I came over? What are we going to wear?"

"Oh Taj please! I know whatever you have in your bag is party worthy and I can cut up some jeans and find a cute top. Now are we going or not?"

"Sure," Taj answered with hesitation.

She definitely wanted to go to the party. This party wasn't like the last one that Amara had missed. This party was being given by one of their classmate's brother that was in college so it would be a lot of older people there. Taj was used to it and knew she could handle herself but she wasn't too sure about Amara. Only time would tell.

***

Saturday night was here and just like Amara said by ten o'clock, everyone was sleep. Taj had some leggings and a shirt with the back out in her bag, Amara had cut and ripped up some jeans and decided to wear just a bra with them. The bra had a floral print on it, so it could pass for a bikini top. It wasn't that hot outside at night so Amara wore a blazer with her outfit.

Amara curled both of their hair, and Taj did their make-up. Once they were almost ready, Taj called the cab so that he would be waiting when they were ready for their big escape. Amara couldn't believe she was actually about to pull this off. Twenty minutes later the cab driver called to them he was outside like they had requested him to do. Amara couldn't risk the sound of a blaring horn waking up her grandparents.

They took their shoes off and walked carefully down the stairs. Amara thought it would be best to go out the backdoor and just leave it unlocked. That way the least amount of noise possible would be made. Once they were inside the cab the put their shoes back on and they were off to party.

Amara looked over at Taj, "We did it!"

"Yes! So far so good. You ready to party?"

"Yeah, but I'm really nervous too. Just make sure we don't get separated okay?"

"Why are you nervous? This was your idea!"

"Yeah I know, but I have never done anything like this before."

"Well I don't have to sneak out, but these parties are really just a bunch of us hanging around and dancing. Some people may be drinking or smoking, but if that's not your thing they won't pressure you into doing it. If you decide to drink just be careful."

"Oh I'm not drinking but ok. Thank you, I feel a little better now."

The rest of the ride was silent, both girls were in their thoughts, and the cab driver didn't have any music playing. Amara was thinking again that this may have been another bad idea. She was getting that feeling she always got when something bad was going to happen. She thought to pray, but then again would God even be able to hear her when she was being disobedient?

They had been driving for about 45 minutes already and Amara could tell they had entered into the suburbs once they got off the freeway because there were no street lights. The GPS from the front seat told the cab driver to continue straight for five miles. It was so dark outside Amara could hardly see, but she could tell that the houses were widely spaced out.

Finally they saw light. The mini mansion was lit up and looked like it was sitting in the middle of the block all by itself. The gate around it made Amara think about the White House. Taj paid the cab driver and they got out. The music was blaring and they were cars lined up in the driveway. Taj's high heels were clicking as they walked up the driveway. Amara had chosen some ballerina flats; she had to be prepared for anything.

When they got to the door, Amara recognized a lot of the guys face from school. Suddenly she realized that Dontay might be here. Amara never heard Dontay talk about parties, but he had been at the last one. Oh well what was she worried about, they were just friends.

"Hey cutie let me talk to you," a very fine guy grabbed Amara.

Taj saw what was about to go down so she told the guy let her talk to her friend first right quick and she would bring her right back. He felt like that was a line, but he let Amara's hand go.

"Look I forgot to tell you the most important rules at these parties. Never tell anyone your age, they are not going to ask but don't volunteer the information. It will get us kicked out. I'm not telling you to do something you don't want to do, but don't act inexperienced either. Got it?"

Amara was really starting to feel out of her element, but she had wanted to come so now she had to act the part. Good thing she had been watching reality shows because she had never been to anything besides a kiddie party in a backyard.

Her and Taj went back to find the guy they had promised to come back to. He was standing in the same spot so Taj let know she would be on the other side of the room but still in her eyesight. His face lit up when he saw Amara walking towards him.

"Hey you really came back!"

Amara smiled and began her performance, "I told I would."

"Great, so what's your name?"

"Amara, yours?"

"Nate"

"Nice to meet you."

"Likewise, so you drink or smoke? You look like you need to relax."

Uh-oh here came the test. Would Amara look inexperienced if she said no? What if she said yes but got too drunk? Oh why did she think this would be a good idea? Before she could answer she felt someone grab her from behind and immediately she knew who it was.

"Hey Nate, you trying to steal my girl?"

"Oh shit Tay, I ain't know this was you. My bad!"

Nate walked away in a hurry like he was scared that Dontay was going to hurt him or something. Dontay turned Amara around and just stared at her. He tried to keep his eyes on her face, but he couldn't help but to look at her breast spilling out of the bra she had on.

"Amara where are your clothes? Why are you here?"

Dontay always had a way of Amara feeling like a three year old that has disappointed her parents, which angered her.

"I got on clothes and what are you doing here?"

"This is my brother's party!"

Oh my goodness Amara was going to strangle Taj! How could she have forgotten to tell her that information?

"Oh!"

"Right so once again, what are you doing here? Does your grandmother know you're here? I will answer that myself, no she doesn't. Let's go, I am taking you home."

"No you are not! You are not my father Dontay."

"Yes I am! I know I am not your father, but I am your friend. Who are you even here with?"

Taj appeared as soon as the question left his mouth.

"She is here with me."

"Wow Taj, you know these parties aren't for Amara. Hell you shouldn't even be here."

"I am tired of everyone acting like I am so fucking fragile or something! I am not leaving and matter of fact, I'm about to go get me something to drink!"

Amara stomped away in frustration. Why did Dontay think it was okay for him to party, but not her? She knew he was older but goodness she wasn't in elementary school. Dontay grabbed her once again.

"Amara I am not playing with you, let's go!"

"No!"

"Amara please don't make me cause a scene. You should not be here and I am taking you home, now! I would never be able to forgive myself if something happened to you. Taj, come on."

Taj couldn't care less, she really only came because Amara wanted to come. Sure she had mentioned the party, but it was just for sake of conversation she didn't think that Amara would bring it back up. Taj truly did not know it was Dontay's brother who was giving the party. She would have never even mentioned it if she knew that.

The girls agreed to leave with Dontay, and actually Amara was so glad that he was there. They hadn't thought about or planned how they would get back home. Amara's face was filled with shock when Dontay hit the alarm on an all-black 2015 Impala.

THE SEARCH FOR AMARA

"Is this your car?"

"Why?"

"Just asking, geesh!"

Dontay clearly had an attitude. When he unlocked the doors, Amara got in the backseat. Taj was confused, but she was not going to sit up front with Dontay while her girl sat in the back. Even though they both kept telling everyone that they were just friends, Taj knew how they felt about each other. So she climbed in the back with Amara.

"Amara get up in the front, what is wrong with you?"

Amara was pouting, so she chose to ignore Dontay.

"Yeah ok, well Taj come up front. Your friend can sit in the back like a two year old."

"Naw I'm good."

"Fine!"

Dontay turned up his radio and started backing out of the driveway. He glanced in the rearview mirror at Amara. She looked so grown, but he could see the true her and she was very naive to the world she was trying so hard to become a part of. It was obvious that Amara was a sheltered child, and even though she had been involved in some crazy situations she had not yet experienced life.

Dontay didn't what it was about her, but he really liked her. He being sixteen and she being twelve was a huge problem for some people, which was the main reason he was only claiming her as his friend.

Taj sang along with the songs being played, while Amara stared out the window until she dozed off. Taj was waking her up shortly letting her know that they were back at the house. Amara opened her eyes and gathered her belongings. She got out the car and started walking to the back of the house without even saying goodbye to Dontay. Taj just shook her head and chuckled while getting out of the car. "When are y'all going to stop this game?" Taj asked Dontay. "It's not a game. Amara is too young and you know it!" "Well then leave her alone." "I can't." "Wow you have to figure out something." "I know that Taj, trust me I know." "Alright, thanks for the ride. I will try to talk to her." "No problem and thanks." Amara was standing by the back door waiting for Taj; she didn't want to open the door more than once. They entered together and quietly closed the door behind them. Amara signaled for Taj to wait before walking up the back stairs. It had been an eventful night. Amara piled her hair in a ponytail on top of her head and went to wash the makeup off her face before she fell in the bed. It was almost 1 o'clock in the morning, and she knew her grandmother was going to make her go to church. Taj had spread out her covers on the floor and went to sleep without washing her face, or even taking off her clothes.

CHAPTER FIFTEEN

With everything that was going on, Amara had forgotten about her order until Dontay bought it to her house one day about a month later. When she had placed the order, they told her the wait was about four to six weeks. Dontay tried to pry to find out what was in the box. Amara refused to engage him in conversation and she had really been limiting her involvement with him since that night at the party.

Dontay was good at constantly pointing out that Amara was too young, yet he still wanted to act like her man. Amara wasn't having it. She was starting to slip back into a state of depression. The diet pills weren't working as quickly as they promised. Or at least that's how Amara felt, but her grandmother was getting worried. She noticed the rapid weight loss, she wasn't going to say anything at first, but when people started pointing out to her she decided that something needed to be said.

When Amara came downstairs one Saturday morning her grandmother was sitting at the table. It was a nice spring day outside. Amara was in a good mood because it was almost time for spring break and her grandparents were taking her and DJ to California. She was still waiting to see if Lysa, Lace, and Taj would be able to go.

"Amara honey sit down we need to talk."

Amara's heart started beating so hard, she felt like she was about to pass out. She couldn't handle any more bad news.

"Grandma did something happened to my mother?"

"Oh honey I didn't mean to frighten you. As far as I know, your mother is fine. We need to talk about you."

"Me?"

"Yes please sit down," Alicia said while patting the chair next to her.

Amara walked over and sat down, she had no idea what her grandmother wanted to talk about.

"Amara I have noticed some changes in you and they are worrying me. I know this is a sensitive subject because most women do not like talking about their weight. However as your grandmother I have to tell you that baby you are losing too much weight. Is everything alright?"

Amara looked at her grandmother like she had grown another head out of her neck.

"Grandma what are you talking about. I NEED to lose weight; I got fat over the winter."

Oh my this is bigger than I imagined Alicia thought.

"Amara you think you are FAT?"

"Grandma you don't have to be nice. I know I picked up a lot of weight, but I'm getting it back off by the summer time."

"Amara honey you are not, were you ever fat! Where did you get that nonsense from?"

THE SEARCH FOR AMARA

Amara was tired of this conversation.

"Grandma do you have anything else you need to talk about?"

Alicia knew that Amara was about to blow up, so she let Amara end the conversation.

"Amara I see you about to step into the disrespectful lane so I'm just going to stop this conversation for now. Delilah is coming to get DJ, so I'm going to get him dressed."

"Why?"

"Huh, why what?"

"Why is Delilah coming to get DJ? And is mommy going to change his name, since he is not a junior?"

"Amara get your little disrespectful self out of my face and you know you better not ever let your mother hear you say that!"

Amara rolled her eyes and went to her room. She called Lace once she got in her bed and back under her covers.

"Hey Amara."

"Hey Lace, why is your momma coming to get my little brother?"

"Whoa what's your deal this morning?"

"Your momma! What is she coming to get DJ for? He ain't y'all family!"

"Amara, where is all of this coming from?"

"Lace we all know that DJ is not Dwayne's baby, so why is your mother still playing the nice auntie role?"

Lace feelings were hurt. Yes her mother sometimes got on her nerves, but the things that Amara was saying were just outright mean!

"Amara do you remember when I first met you?"

"Yeah and?"

"Do you remember how my grandparents welcomed you?"

If Amara was in her right state of mind she would have gotten the point that Lace was making, and she would have felt bad. Right now however, Amara was dealing with a lot of different emotions, mainly anger so she was not thinking clearly.

"Lace whatever, they knew I wasn't family. I just asked a simple question. What is your momma coming over here to get DJ for? You know she always has an ulterior motive!"

"Amara I don't know what is going on with you this morning, but I am not going to talk to you right now or later if you continue to act like this. Goodbye."

Amara laughed and ended the call. She hadn't been on any social media in weeks so she opened up Facebook first to see what everyone was talking about. Taj had just made a status six minutes ago and already it had fifteen likes. People were funny. All the status said was that she was bored and hungry. A comment popped up from someone named 'NateTheGR8' *let me come get you,* he offered. Amara kept scrolling down and then stopped when she saw a post from 'Tay'sWorld' which was Dontay's Facebook name, *Why does life have to be so hard-Feeling confused.* Amara clicked like and scrolled back up to see if Taj had responded to her offer.

Amara clicked on the name to see the person's pictures. Taj hadn't told her about any new boyfriends, and they talked almost every day about almost everything. Amara was a little bit jealous when she saw that it was the boy that had tried to talk to her at the party. Going back to the status, Taj had commented *LOL, yeah oh, come get me then :-)*. Oh so Taj must have been feeling him, which would explain why she was so eager when Dontay made them leave.

Amara sent Dontay a text message first asking him why was he feeling confused. Then she sent Taj a text message next asking her what was she doing. Dontay text back and asked her did she want to go sit at the park. That sounded like a good idea so she told him she would be ready in 20 minutes.

She got up and hurried to shower and put on something comfortable. When she got out the shower, she heard loud voices coming from downstairs while she was lotioning up before she put on her clothes. She had just put her socks and was getting ready to brush her hair when she heard her name being called.

"AMARA get your behind down here!"

"What now?" Amara said as she walked out her room.

Entering the kitchen, she wanted to go back upstairs. Delilah was sitting at the table in full performance mode. She tissues piled up in front of her but her eyes were not red and her face was barely wet.

"Yes grandma."

"What is your problem little girl?"

"What did I do now" Amara asked throwing her hands up in the air. She wanted to slap Delilah for getting her yelled at.

"Did you not think that Lace was going to tell her mother what you said to her?"

Amara rolled her eyes and sighed, "Oh I didn't say anything wrong. I mean Delilah why are you over here?" she turned around and asked her. "Amara that is enough!" Alicia intervened. The spirit of bitterness had a stronghold over Amara and it was becoming worse and worse. "Listen here young lady. First and foremost I do not owe your spoiled ass an explanation if I want to come get my nephew! You don't have authority around here." Amara clapped her hands, "Good job are you done?" Alicia stood up and slapped Amara across her face so hard, Amara's face immediately turned red. This was getting out of hand. She would talk with Delilah in private, right now was not the time. However calling Amara out of her name was not acceptable either. "Amara go upstairs. Delilah, DJ is ready to go let me go get him from his grandfather." Delilah was in shock but she was glad that Alicia had slapped Amara, she had wanted to do it for months but she knew it was cause a problem. Amara marched upstairs, she couldn't believe that her grandmother had just slapped her, but she

THE SEARCH FOR AMARA

was not staying in this house. She only went upstairs to get her phone and her keys. When she came back downstairs she went out the front door, slamming it behind her so that her grandparents knew without a doubt that she had left. She knew it would be consequences when she came back, but she had to get out of this house before she snapped.

CHAPTER SIXTEEN

She had sent Dontay a message and told him to just meet her at the park, it wasn't that far and she was not waiting for him to come get her. Walking to the park was allowing her to calm down a little bit, but it was also giving her idle mind time to reflect on all the wrong things that were going on in her life. Those thoughts were causing her to get mad again.

Her phone started ringing and when she saw it was her mother, she sent her right to voicemail. Amara didn't hear anything her mother had to say. She decided that she was not taking any more phone calls or responding to anymore text message from her. If her mother wanted to talk to her, she would have to come back home and talk face to face.

When she reached the park, she walked over to one of the picnic tables and sat on the table. Dontay text her and told her that she should have waited and he would be pulling up in less than a minute. Taj text back telling her to call her. Then her phone started going crazy with notifications. Her mother had sent her a long text message which resulted in six messages coming through. Amara refused to even read the messages right now.

Dontay pulled up and stepped out the car looking so darn good. Amara wished the she was older. It was nothing worse than liking a good looking boy who looked at you like a little sister. Whenever Amara would try to distance herself from him, he would tell her that she wasn't being a good friend. It was like he would guilt trip her back into talking to him.

Amara sent Taj a quick text that she would call her later. She didn't even realize she was smiling so hard until Dontay asked her what was she so happy about when he gave her hug. He then sat down on the table next to her and just stared up at the sky.

"Amara what's going with you?"

"Nothing"

"Oh yeah? I just got a call from your grandmother. I didn't want to say anything but she said she had already brought up this issue this morning. I could literally feel your ribs when you gave me hug. Your grandmother also said that you have been very disrespectful lately."

"Oh Lord, here we go again. Dontay you can't be both. I need a friend, not a father!"

"Amara that is what you keep missing. I only talk to this way because I am your friend. I don't talk to like this just because I am older than you. Real friends don't want to see their friends in trouble or hurt. They tell them the hardcore truth even when they don't want to hear it."

Amara felt like Dontay was what people called an old soul. He was so cute, but at the same time he acted like a grandfather. She didn't want to hear what he was saying so she changed the subject.

"Ok I hear you. So anyway what are you confused about?"

Dontay began to share his future plans. He had already applied to several colleges and was awaiting acceptance letters. He planned to major in Psychology and open his own practice. He had already applied to colleges in New York, Connecticut, Pennsylvania, and Michigan.

Amara listened and was impressed that he had his future mapped out. Most kids their age did know what they were going to do, until forced them to think about it. She was also amazed that as much as they had talked, they had never talked about their shared interest in Psychology. Amara told him that she was going to New York to study at Columbia University when she graduated high school.

They talked a little while longer about school until Dontay switched back to the earlier topic. Dontay told Amara that he understood her frustration but she needed to go home and apologize to her grandparents. Amara said that she would but she still just needed a break and asked him could he drop her off at Taj's house. Dontay said he would but she had to call her grandmother.

Amara called her grandmother and apologized, but told her she thought it would be best if she calmed down for a couple of days. Her grandmother said absolutely not and she better bring herself home right away. Amara was glad that she had remembered to turn her volume. Her grandmother had been hung up but Amara kept talking like she was on the phone still.

"Well my grandmother is not happy but she agreed. She said she will come pick me up tomorrow."

"Alright cool. Well since I'm taking to Taj's you want to hang out a little while longer?"

"Sure!"

They sat on the table and talked until the sun started going down and it started getting chilly. Dontay had turned off his ringer because he didn't want any interruptions while he was with Amara. The more he talked to her, the more it was easier to forget her age. If he would have had checked his phone he would have saw that Alicia had called ten times.

They walked to the car and decided to stop at McDonald's on the way to Taj's house. Amara called Taj and asked if she wanted anything. She said just get her a McDouble and a small fry. When they reached Taj's house neither one of them wanted to separate but Dontay promised to call Amara before he went to sleep. He got the car and walked her to the door carrying her bags. While they were waiting for Taj to come open the door, Dontay leaned in and kissed Amara on the lips and then on her cheek.

Amara started blushing and smiling, "Where did that come from?"

"I'm sorry, I couldn't help myself."

Taj opened the door and let them in. Well Amara came in, Dontay handed her the bags and said he had to go. Amara and Taj went and got settled at the table to eat. Amara was glad to know that Taj's parents were out of town, so it would be just them. Amara would never be able to get used to having cameras around watching her every move.

They finished eating and went upstairs to Taj's room. Amara reached in her pocket to check her phone, when she noticed the battery had died. She plugged it up and went to sit on the bed with Taj.

Taj started telling her about her new relationship with Nate. They had actually been talking since the day after the party. Taj was so caught up in her story; she didn't notice the look on Amara's face. Amara couldn't control her jealousy anymore.

"Did you forget that he tried to talk to me first?"

Taj was caught off guard and didn't know how to respond.

"I know you remember him from the party?"

"Yeah but since you didn't talk to him, I didn't think it would be a problem."

"Yeah I didn't talk to him because Dontay interfered.

"Wow Amara, really?"

"Yes really! Who said I didn't like Nate?"

"Amara that is not fair, you have Dontay."

"I don't have Dontay. He acts like my father!"

"Dontay loves you Amara, he is just scared because of your age."

"Scared of what though?"

"Amara I know 4 years doesn't seem like a lot to you, and if you were over 18 it wouldn't really matter at all. But you are only about to be thirteen and he is sixteen. To a lot of people that is major."

Amara was so used to being around people older than her, and a lot of times she forgot that people still saw her as a little girl. Truthfully at 12, that was what she was.

"Yeah ok but anyway back to Nate."

"Amara look we can talk about Nate, but I don't owe you an explanation. Nate was not yours, and you did not talk to him. You had a conversation, and Dontay shut it down."

"Ha! Now I see that Sky had told some truth, so did you give Nate some of your goodies already?"

"WHAT! Amara you know what, you need to call Dontay because you have to go. Matter of fact I will call him for you."

"Yeah whatever!"

Taj ignored Amara and went to get her phone off the dresser to call Dontay who was shockingly calling her.

"Hello"

"Hey Taj, sorry to interrupt but can you put Amara on the phone she is not answering hers."

"Oh I can do even better than that! You need to come back and get her out of my house!"

"Wait what happened?"

"She is over being very rude and disrespectful! You have to come get your girl or she's just going to be sitting outside."

"Ok Taj, I'm on my way back anyway. She didn't tell me that her grandmother told her to come home. I never would have brought her over there if I would have known that."

"Wow, ok."

Taj hung up the phone and looked over at Amara who was checking notifications on her phone.

"Oh so you talking to Dontay too now? How did he get your number?"

"Amara get yo life! He was looking for you and he is on his way back. Dontay probably got my number from his friend, you know Nate! Take your stuff and go sit on the porch. I can't believe you came over here and showed your ass! Get out of my house, and do not speak to me unless you are offering a sincere apology."

Amara grabbed her phone and charger and walked out the room and down the stairs out the house. She was not going to sit on Taj's porches. She put her grandmother's address in her GPS on her phone and started walking in the correct direction. She text Dontay and told him she would be walking.

Luckily for her, Dontay was closer than Amara thought. She had only been walking for five minutes when she saw Dontay's Impala. She got in ready to hear the lecture she was sure Dontay was about to give her. Much to her surprise, Dontay remained silent.

THE SEARCH FOR AMARA

The darkness of the night and the soft jazz were slowly putting Amara to sleep. Dontay looked over and wished he could know what was going on in Amara's mind. In the short time that he had known her, she was making drastic changes for the worse.

He knew that Mrs. Alicia kept her in church, and the little bit that he knew about church he couldn't understand why Amara was acting so horribly. He focused back on the road so that he could get her back to her grandmother safely.

Dontay was even more confused now. He had just decided that he didn't care what people thought and Amara was mature for her age, but this move had been very immature and not acceptable. She didn't talk about her mother much, but maybe her absence is what was causing Amara to act like this.

Dontay couldn't believe that the little feisty, very smart, and very mature girl sitting next to him was only twelve. She behaved like a sixteen year old, and staring at her she even looked like one. He had to constantly remind himself that she was much too young for him. Dontay pulled up in the driveway and didn't have any words to say to Amara as she got out of the car.

Amara wanted to be anyway but here, but she might as well hurry up in the house to suffer the consequences so she could go to bed. Walking in she expected her grandmother to be waiting for her, she almost passed out when her mother was standing in the middle of the kitchen with a belt in her hand.

"Mom!"

"Yeah I knew you wouldn't read those messages. Get your behind in here."

Before Amara could say anything, her mother started giving her a butt whoopin that would go down in history. Amara felt like her breath was being sucked out of her body, she had been screaming for so long.

"Asha that is enough!" Henry shouted coming into the kitchen.

Asha was so frustrated though with everything that was going on and all the bad reports she had been getting about her child's behavior; she didn't even hear her father screaming at her to stop.

Alicia came in and grabbed Asha tightly and said in her ear, "Asha that is enough."

Asha dropped the belt and collapsed in the middle of the floor. Even though Amara had been acting so out of order, Asha had took all of her frustration out on her. That whoopin had bordered on the thin line of child abuse.

***

After the night they had experienced, nobody was able to get up to go to church. Even though that was the best place to be in a time like this, they physically were not able. Amara thought her body was sore when she got jumped, but that was nothing compared to this pain.

Asha had stayed up all night talking to her parents about what had been going on and where she had been. It turned out that Asha had been going back and forth to interviews and was trying to decide if she wanted to move out of the state if she was offered the position. Once the results had come back that Dwayne was not the father, it made her decision a little easier. Then she thought about her parents and how moving Amara again would affect her, so she had turned down the position and she would not be leaving anymore. Her parents still could not believe that Asha had actually cheated on Dwayne. Especially after that had happened between them, but her parents would not dwell on the past.

CHAPTER SEVENTEEN

The end of the school year was a couple of months away and things were beginning to get back to some normalcy. Amara was back in her house, in her room, with her stuff. She was so upset with herself because her behavior had caused her to miss out on going to Orlando for spring break. Her and Taj had repaired their relationship, and were actually closer now than they were before. They were back hanging out, and sometimes her, Taj, Nate and Dontay would all hang out together.

Lace and Amara were still not talking because Amara refused to apologize for telling the truth. Asha told her daughter that her stubbornness might backfire on her one day and life was too short, but Amara was still not trying to hear it. Lysa would come over on some weekends, and through all the craziness Lysa was the only one Amara had not experienced an argument with.

Just when things seemed to be calming down, Amara had that sense of the calm before the storm again. Even though she had picked her appetite back up, she was still taking the diet pills. She had gained a little weight back so that she didn't look sick. The weight was ok with her though because she was still less than 130 pounds.

She was excited to be spending the night at Lysa's. They had plans though to go a party with Taj. This party was more their age group, but with celebrity parents it was guaranteed to be a lot of adult like behavior going on. Amara was just glad that her mother had restored her privileges.

Amara was looking through her clothes trying to figure out what she was going to wear. She rarely wore skirts except to church, but since it was spring, she looked for a cute dress in her closet. Her notifications had her phone dancing on her dresser. Earlier when she was finishing up her homework, she had put it on vibrate.

Although her mother had restored her privileges, she still didn't play about her grades. The first sign in grade slippage immediately got something taken away. Amara had already experience it once, when her mother took her tablet because her grade in History has slipped a little bit taking her from a low A, to a high B. Now to most parents a B would still be considered good. Asha knew what her daughter was capable of so she didn't accept anything but A's.

When she finally found the dress she was looking for she laid it on her bed, walked over to her dresser, turned the ringer back on first, and then checked her notifications. The first ones she read were her Facebook notifications. She hated when people tagged her in stuff. Even though she had to accept it, it still showed up on whoever's timeline that had tagged her.

Opening it up she almost dropped her phone when she saw that the person who had tagged her in a post was Sky. When she looked at the post, it was a check-in showing that Sky was back in

Tampa. She had tagged a few other people also, but Amara noticed that she hadn't tagged Taj. Amara started to comment, but she didn't even know what to say so instead she called Taj before checking the other notifications.

"What's up girlie?"

"Taj have you been on Facebook today?"

"Not really, what's going on?"

"Sky tagged me in a check-in that shows her in Tampa."

"Oh wow, is she trying to be funny?"

"I don't know, I was thinking the same thing!"

"Well if she know what's good she will make sure we don't see her."

"Right! What you doing?"

"Waiting for my hair stylist to get here."

"Oh okay, yeah I went to the shop yesterday. Another benefit I was missing out on when my mother was gone."

"Girl I know that was killing you, but you got skills yourself. Have you ever thought about doing hair?"

"Professionally? No. I don't have patience that is why I hate doing my own. It is fun to do every now and then, but I would never do hair all day for a living."

"It does seem like a lot of work. Anyway about our night, you and Lysa are still coming with me right?"

"Yes we are. She just sent me a message on Kik, but I had my phone on vibrate earlier when I was doing my work and forgot to turn the ringer back on. I was just checking my notifications when I saw that Sky was back in the city, so immediately called you before I checked any other notifications."

"Oh okay well go finish getting ready and call me if anything changes."

"Okay see you soon."

Amara ended the call and went back to her notifications. She had several notifications on her Kik app so she opened it next before she looked at her missed calls. She opened her conversation with Lysa first, just in case something had changed that she needed to handle right away.

The messages were not urgent, just the usual what are you doing, what are you wearing, and what time her and her dad would be there to pick her up. Amara replied back that she was wearing a dress and she would be ready when she got to her house. She asked Lysa were they still going to the party. Lysa immediately replied back of course! Amara was happy because she didn't want to miss the party.

She saw a notification from Dontay but decided to give him a call. She put the phone a speaker so she could still be checking what he had sent while she was waiting for him to answer. It was just a simple message the he had been thinking about her all morning. He answered right before it went to voicemail.

"Hey darling!"

"Darling," Amara asked with a smirk on her face, "like seriously how old are you?"

"Too old! What you doing?"

"Nothing just finished my work not too long ago, now I'm getting my stuff together for tonight."

"Tonight? What is going on tonight? You cheating on me already?"

"Tay you are mess, you know I told you I was spending the night at Lysa's and we are going to the party."

"Oh I guess I remember you telling me something like that. So what are you wearing? Do I need to show up and be your security?"

"Nope not my security, but you do need to show up and be my man."

"Oh is that right? I may slide through; I have to see what my brother had planned for tonight. He told my dad earlier that he was coming by tonight."

"That's fine, if you don't make it. You know I will see you tomorrow at my grandma's for Sunday dinner."

"I don't miss those Sundays for nothing and nobody. So you know I will be there."

Amara and Dontay continued their conversation talking about nothing really important, just spending time on the phone. Like teenagers used to do. Most teens now want to just text, Kik, or snapchat. Teens rarely talk anymore. Dontay had told Amara that all though she was young he was still making her his girl. He promised that he respected her too much to take things any further than them just talking and hanging out. Dontay had won Alicia's heart and love. She wanted nothing more than to see her granddaughter marry him in her future. He had even started coming to their church and got his parents to come. His mother was coming every Sunday and his father came every Sunday that he didn't have to work. Asha loved Dontay too; he was a great influence on her daughter. She just didn't believe that Amara was old enough for a boyfriend no matter how old he was. It seemed like her mother had a tendency to forget that Amara was only going on thirteen years old.

Amara ended the call so she could finish getting everything together and go downstairs. She wanted to play with her little brother for a little while before she left. She had folded her dress that she was wearing to the party up and put it in her bag. The dress that she was taking to wear to church tomorrow, she had placed in her garment bag.

She gathered her stuff to go downstairs, right before she flipped the switch to turn off her light; she remembered that her charger was still plugged up. She had too much in her hand so she decided to take it downstairs and then come back up to get it. DJ came flying to the steps when he heard coming down.

"Sissy!" he said in such an adorable voice.

"Mommy can you come get him? I have too much stuff in my hand and I don't want to trip over him. "

"DJ!" Asha called from the living room, "DJ!"

He turned towards the way he heard his name be called from, took one last look at Amara, and took off running and laughing with his little chubby legs.

Amara reached the front hallway and put her stuff on the table next to the door, and ran back up the stairs to get her charger. She also remembered when she got in her room that she hadn't taken her pill today or yesterday. They didn't say anything about taking two pills in one day, so she decided to take two before she left. The plans were go to eat tonight before the party and she didn't want to have worry about her stomach being all huge in her dress tonight at the party.

Even though Amara's behavior as far as being disrespectful and snapping on people had been totally changed for the best, she still had her moments of depression and she was still very conscious about her self-image. Coming out of the bathroom after taking her pills, she grabbed her charger, and made her way back downstairs.

DJ came running to the bottom of the stairs again, but this time she tucked her charger in her hoodie pocket and picked him up. She tickled his stomach while lifting him up in the air. Nothing melted her heart more than to hear a baby brother's laugh. Time was going fast and he was advanced. He wasn't even quite one yet and he was already talking clearly. Amara put him down and then pretended to be running from him, so he would follow her back into the living room. He couldn't stop laughing and he was running behind her with a look of determination though. When she got in the living room she let him grab her and fell on the floor. Asha just sat back and viewed her kids. She was so happy and proud of her little family.

She was hurt that her and Dwayne didn't work out, but hey that was life. Asha would be just fine with her two babies whom she adored. Amara looked over at her and smiled.

"Mommy I love you."

"I love you too child, what you want?"

"Dang momma! Why do parents always think that their kids want something just because we tell y'all we love you? I'm not saying it anymore."

"Whatever little big head girl. What time is Lysa coming to pick you up?"

"She is on her way now, which is why I came downstairs. I wanted to play with my brother too."

"Aww I am so proud of your relationship with your brother. I was worried how you would interact with him. I wondered how you would welcome a new baby after being the only child for so long. I'm so sorry that I messed up Amara. I knew that you were looking forward to have a father figure in your life."

"Mommy all is forgiven. I will always have grandpa as an example. I feel worse for you and Dwayne than myself. I'm just glad you are back home and things are getting back to normal." Before Asha could respond, Amara's phone started ringing. "This is Lysa calling, she must be pulling up." "Hello, I'm outside." "Ok here I come." "I love you mommy. Are you coming to church tomorrow?" "Depends on how DJ acts in the morning. If not, you know I will be over grandma's for Sunday dinner." Amara walked over to give DJ a hug and a kiss before she left. He had learned something new. Today he grabbed her neck and kissed her cheek making a loud smooching noise. Amara and Asha both burst out laughing. Their laughter made DJ laugh and do it again. Amara hugged him again kissed her mother on the cheek.

CHAPTER EIGHTEEN

Lysa's dad had taken the girls to Golden Corral. Amara was glad she took two diet pills because she planned to definitely eat all that she could eat. When they finally decided to call it quits, Amara almost started to go make herself throw up. She felt as if she had gained twenty pounds. When they got in the car, Amara laid her head back on the headrest and must have dozed off.

She heard Lysa laughing and calling her name, "Amara girl you are snoring loud!"

Amara sat up and looked around trying to figure out where they were. She had forgotten that Lysa had moved, so she really had no idea where they were at. She looked at the window trying to see if she saw anything familiar. After a few minutes she gave up and pulled out her phone. She wasn't trying to go to sleep again.

She sent Dontay a message to see where he was at and what was he doing. This is one reason Amara loved Kik, the messages were instant. He responded that he was about to go play basketball with his brother and some friends. He asked where she was at. Amara told him that she was almost to Lysa's house. She decided not to ask him if he was still coming to the party, she didn't want to be disappointed and ruin the mood later.

He responded as if he was reading her mind. He told her that his brother had just come over to hang out and go play basketball. When they were finished he was going to ride with Nate and come to the party. Amara was so happy that Dontay would be at the party.

"Amara are you sleeping again?"

"No!"

"I called your name like five times"

Lysa's dad shook his head, "Lysa now you know you are exaggerating."

"Dad hush."

Finally they got to Lysa's and now Lysa was exaggerating acting like she was sleepy so that her parents wouldn't come check on them.

"Goodnight daddy, after that delicious dinner, we are stuffed and ready to hit those pillows."

"Ok Lysa, I get the hint! I won't come bother you all. Your mom is already in the bed so I will see you both bright and early in the morning for church."

"Goodnight Mr. Payne."

"Goodnight Amara."

He went down the hall to the other side of the house, and the girls ran up the stairs to Lysa's room.

"Lysa you are absolutely one of the luckiest girls in the world. You live in this huge house, and you are basically on one whole side by yourself!"

"Yeah for the most part, except for when my sister is home from college. The silence is good most of the time, but sometimes it is creepy."

"Yeah I would probably be scared too sometimes, and bored. I was the only child for so long but now I wouldn't trade my baby brother for nothing in the world."

"I'm about to go take a shower to wake myself up. You can turn on the television or whatever. Make yourself at home. Mi casa es su casa!" Lysa said while giggling and dancing out of the room.

***

The girls had made a successful escape. With Lysa's parents being on the other side of the house and asleep, it hadn't really taken much effort. Once they walked around the corner, Amara sent Taj a Kik message asking her where was she at. Taj replied telling her to turn around.

Amara turned around and immediately she felt her mouth form the hugest smile. Taj was sitting in the passenger seat of Nate's car which meant that Dontay was in the back. Amara started feeling bad, because she didn't want Lysa to feel like an outsider.

"I'm so sorry Lysa I didn't know until the last minute that Nate and Dontay were coming together, we can stay home if you want. "

"No way, maybe I can find a boyfriend too at the party."

Amara was glad that Lysa didn't say yes. She really wanted to go to the party, plus she really wanted to spend time with Dontay. She got in the backseat excited and scooted as close to Dontay as possible. Lysa climbed in behind her. Dontay wrapped his arm around Amara pulling her tight for a hug, and they were off to the party.

When they pulled up to the house, there were not any outside lights on and it was really quiet. Nate put the car in park. Turning towards the backseat, he asked Dontay,

"You want to go knock, they may have canceled the party?"

"Yeah it is too quiet, but let's go check it out."

Both guys kissed their girlfriends and got out the car, before they got to the door someone started pulling the door open. A girl that Nate recognized as a sophomore waved her hand telling them to come in.

"We have three girls in the car, can they come in too?"

"Do they go to our school?"

"Two of them do."

"Who is the other one?"

"She is my girlfriend's friend," Dontay answered.

"Your girlfriend!" the girl asked with a voice full of aggravation, "who is your girlfriend?"

"Amara."

"Amara!" the girl squealed, "I love her! Yes tell her to get in here."

Dontay went back to the car to get the girls, telling Amara she had a fan waiting for her in the house. Once everyone was out of the car, Nate turned the alarm on.

Taj walked into the house first; follow by Lysa, and lastly Amara. When Amara entered the door, the girl grabbed her and pulled her into a tight hug. Even though Dontay had warned her, Amara was still taken back by the girl's behavior. The girl, who finally introduced herself as Zoe, led them down a hallway and to the back of the house.

Amara was staring at the pictures on the wall, and was trying to hold in her amazement. Judging by the pictures and the plaques lining the walls, they were in the house of the biggest music producer. Lysa grabbed her hand and they both just smiled at each other.

Finally they reached a set of double doors. When Zoe opened the door, it was like they were about to enter another dimension. The room was cloudy like someone was smoking. The room was pitch black with neon lights flashing. The music was shaking the floor beneath their feet when they fully stepped in the room.

All of their eyes were open with shock and amazement. Even Taj had never experienced anything like this before. Zoe grabbed Dontay, which caused a glare from Amara.

"This room is soundproof, that is why you couldn't hear anything upstairs. Can I talk to you in private later?"

Dontay just pulled away from Zoe and walked back over to Amara. They looked around for any familiar faces. Not really being able to see anyone, they walked to the other side of the room and took a seat. The room was much bigger than they originally thought. When they sat on the couch, Dontay explained to Amara that the room was soundproof. She turned and explained to everyone else. Lysa saw that there was a space for a dance floor, but it was empty. It was a DJ booth and he was playing Kendrick Lamar, who was Lysa's favorite rapper.

"Well love birds, I am about to get the party started. See ya," Lysa said and danced over to the dance floor.

When the DJ saw that someone was finally actually dancing, he switched up to "Lean and Dab", the hottest new song by some young boy that went by the name iHeartMemphis. That was all it took, almost everyone was up on their feet dancing. Some were on the dance floor, but most had just stood and started dancing.

Lysa was having a good time when a boy came up behind her and started dancing. The DJ then just went into a mix playing all different types of what they called "Turn Up" music. Nate,

THE SEARCH FOR AMARA

Dontay, Taj, and Amara had sat back down but they were still bobbing their heads and throwing their hands up in the air.

Taj asked did they want to try some liquor. Nate was more than ready. Dontay however looked at Amara. He had drinks before with his older brother; mostly beer but he had some experience with liquor too.

"Amara you can drink some wine. It taste practically like juice and I promise you won't get sick" Taj assured her with Dontay and Nate agreeing.

"Sure," Amara answered, she really didn't want to and something (The Holy Spirit) was warning her not to, but she didn't want to seem like a lame.

Looking over to check on Lysa, she even had a cup in her hand so Amara was definitely not going to be the only one not participating in the fun. Nate and Dontay got up and headed to the opposite side of the room where there was an actual bar across the back wall.

Taj was snapping her fingers and rocking back and forth to the beat of some new song by Beyoncé. Amara had never been a Beyoncé fan, and she really was not impressed with her new music. She just sat and looked around the room. She was really trying to figure out why was she here.

Amara was not having fun and wondered what Lace was doing. She would rather been laying across her bed eating snacks and watching a movie she had watched a million times before. She pulled out her phone and was about to send Lace a message when Dontay placed a cup in her face.

Amara smelled first and the drink barely had a smell to it at all. She placed the cup to her lips and took a sip. Taj was right it did taste like white grape juice. Amara looked at Dontay and smiled.

"Do you like it?"

"Yes but is this actually wine? Tay it tastes like juice."

"I know, but yes it is really wine, I watched him pour it."

Amara took another sip and a calm feeling washed over her. She had never even thought of drinking anything besides juice and water, heck she hardly drank pop. However if this was how wine made you feel, she would drink it more often.

Before she knew it the cup was empty. Amara felt so relaxed she didn't want to ever move, but she wanted some more.

"Dontay," she said in a hushed tone, but shockingly he heard her.

"Yes, are you ok?"

"I am feeling good, I want some more."

"Are you sure?"

"Yes."

Dontay took Amara's cup and got up to get her some more. He was starting to worry though. He didn't want Amara to get drunk but he was glad she was enjoying herself. Maybe he could get her to loosen up. He was tired of playing the good boy act. Yes he loved church, but he was also a horny teenage boy. He did love Amara, but he just wanted to be the first to ever feel her.

Dontay hadn't told Amara, but he had been accepted already to two colleges and now he was just trying to decide which one he was going to go to. In the meantime he would be graduating next year and didn't want to leave Amara a virgin for somebody else to take what he craved.

While he was waiting at the bar, Zoe came over and tried to put her arms around him. Dontay moved away, but she kept coming until she had him backed up against a wall.

"Dontay what are you doing with that young little naive girl?"

"Zoe backup out my face please."

Zoe moved back, but she would get Dontay before tonight was over. Dontay stared at her for a minute then walked around her and back to the bar. Before anything else could be said or done, Taj walked up. "Dontay do you need some help?" "Umm naw Taj, I got it." "Yeah ok. Zoe maybe you need some help with something." "Nope. Taj I can get what I want all by myself." Taj got up in Zoe's face and said between clenched teeth, "Don't get fucked up! He is off limits!" "Oh is that right? Well we will see about that," Zoe said smiling and walking away. Taj looked at Dontay hoping that he was serious about Amar. She turned and started walking back over to Dontay and Amara.

CHAPTER NINETEEN

The night ended peacefully with no problems. The guy, who Lysa had started dancing with, had stay up under her all night until it was time for them to go. Amara had two more cups full of wine and had gotten a little tipsy. Taj warned Lysa that Amara would sleep it off and be okay in the morning, just make sure that she drank some orange juice and ate a light meal.

Lysa was glad that Amara was doing well, she on the other hand felt horrible. Lysa had chosen to drink hard liquor trying to impress Mario. He was fun to be around, and Lysa did not want him to walk away if she acted like a little girl that didn't drink. It was a good thing that she didn't look her age, or some might look it like a bad thing for guys like Mario. Mario was nineteen and Lysa had told him she was seventeen.

The girls made it downstairs with just enough time to eat some toast before they went to church. Lysa begged Amara to please go downstairs to the youth service. She didn't want Pastor Rob to call her out if she fell asleep. Amara hated going downstairs because they didn't teach anything but she agreed since she knew Lysa wasn't feeling too well.

Amara was getting frustrated. She couldn't understand how Pastor Rob would pick such boring ministers to be over the youth department. They hadn't gone over one scripture, and half of the kids were on their phones either on Facebook or Instagram. Lysa was pleased that they weren't do anything. She could put her head down and rest.

Finally service was over. At least Amara had Sunday dinner to look forward to. When they got back upstairs, Lysa's dad looked in a hurry so she decided to go home, and told Amara she would call her later on. Asha said she had to go to the store to pick up somethings for DJ, and she would meet them at the house in a little while.

"Well looks like it's just us," Dontay said to Amara and Alicia.

"I guess so, let's go. The food is ready. I just need to put it in the oven for about thirty minutes to warm it up."

They all walked out to Alicia's car and were anxious to get home. Especially Amara, she hadn't eaten since yesterday. She felt Dontay staring at her, so she pulled down the visor to look at him in the mirror. To her surprise he was actually looking out the window.

Amara pushed the visor back up and listened to her grandmother as she sang along with the gospel songs on the radio. Alicia's sweet voice put both Amara and Dontay to sleep. When she pulled in the driveway, Dontay stirred but quickly went back to sleep.

Alicia just sat still for a moment and looked at them. She prayed that they would both remained innocent until they were married, but as corrupted as this world was now and days, that was a large request to ask for.

"Dontay...Amara...wake up."

Both of them woke up, everyone got out of the car, and they entered into the house. Alicia went straight into the kitchen to get started. She cut the oven on, pulled the items out the refrigerator, and then walked to the back of the house in search for Henry.

"Amara are you ok?" Dontay asked trying to stay quiet.

"I am fine!"

"Don't snap at me! I was just concerned since you decided to drink like a fish last night."

"Whatever Dontay, you seemed to be enjoying it right along with me."

Dontay got up and walked outside to sit on the porch. He was tired of being confused. Some decisions needed to be made. He pulled out his phone and opened Instagram. While he was scrolling, a text from Zoe came through asking him what was he doing. Dontay deleted the message and went back to liking pictures. Zoe was determined so she sent another message. This time it was a picture message and he was hesitant about opening it.

When he did he was shocked! Zoe had sent him a picture of her in the mirror with not a piece of clothing on. Dontay did what most young men his age would do. Stared! Zoe hid a nice body under those clothes. Dontay was so busy checking out Zoe's boobs, he didn't even notice that Amara was standing behind him.

"Oh so that's what you want? Ha! That explains everything."

"Amara wait! It is not what you think."

"Oh the oldest line in the book. You must have forgotten who you are talking to. I have probably the highest IQ of everyone you know. What I know, not think is that Zoe sent you a naked picture and you are out here drooling on the screen."

"Amara, I didn't ask Zoe to send me this picture."

"So how did she get your number?"

Dontay was busted there; he did finally give in to Zoe's antics last night and gave her his number. He admits it was dumb, but he wasn't thinking clearly.

"Look Amara, you're right and I'm sorry."

"You know Dontay, it doesn't even matter. All we are is friends right?"

Amara was fed up and now it was time to let the games begin. She turned around and went back in the house, yelling over her shoulder that dinner was ready.

Dontay sat on the stairs a little while longer, feeling like such an idiot.

He went in and tried to enjoy dinner, but it was very hard when Amara wouldn't pay him any attention. Alicia noticed the tension and overheard the argument so she decided to stay out of it.

Everyone sat around the table stuffed, and Dontay said he was about to walk home. Amara was glad, she just wanted to go get in her bed and call her friends. Her grandmother had a strict rule of no electronics at the table. She was staring to get worried about her mother, but before she could call she heard her little brother's laughter.

She wanted to go play with her little brother, but she also just wanted sleep.

"Amara let's go! DJ needs a bath."

"Coming!"

Good they were going home.

***

"No way Amara, she actually sent him a picture with no clothes on?" Lace asked with disbelief in her tone.

Being she was only twelve, she hadn't even had the sex talk yet. Although Asha constantly told Delilah that she needed to make her aware. So in her mind the thought of teenage girls sending naked picture was unheard of.

"Yes Lace! Dang how many times are you going to ask me the same thing? You know what I'll call you back later."

Amara was aggravated. She had called Lace because she didn't want to embarrass herself by telling her friends what had happened. Taj would be ready to fight Zoe, and Lysa would be telling her how stupid she was. She laid back on her bed and started daydreaming.

She began to think if she let Dontay have sex with her, maybe he wouldn't pay attention to Zoe. Or maybe she should get a guy more close to her age and start showing up lots of attention. She was confused. Amara didn't know whether she was supposed to make Dontay mad, or was she supposed to give in.

While she thought about what would happen if she decided to have sex with Dontay, her phone started ringing. Amara picked up the phone to see who was calling. She was hoping that it was Dontay, but she was disappointed when she saw Taj's name.

"Hello."

"Hey girl, where are you?"

"I'm home, what's up?"

"Ummm have you talked to Dontay?"

"Yeah I was just with him a couple of hours ago at my grandma's house."

"Ok, have you checked Facebook lately?"

"Taj you know I hate when you do this! Just tell me what you saw on Facebook, sheesh already."

"Calm down missy. First of all I didn't see anything. I was informed about some activity, and I decided to call my bestie before I investigated."

Amara laughed, wondering when she and Taj became besties. While she was talking to Taj, she was scrolling at the same time. Nothing stood out that caught her attention right away. She was about to give up looking when pictures popped up that immediately pissed her off.

"Taj how could you?"

"Huh? What are you talking about?"

"Obviously you need to go take a look at Facebook!"

"I have been on there since we've been talking, and I didn't see anything that would make you so upset. Are you going to tell me what the problem is? I don't have time for this foolishness!"

"Oh so you don't know about the TBT (Throwback Thursdays) pictures of you and Dontay?"

"Are you serious? That's what all the hype is about? I got a text that there were pictures of Dontay and some girl all over Facebook. I didn't know it was us though."

"Excuse me!"

"Amara I have known Dontay for years, and I told you that. So I'm sure the pictures are of nothing more than us just hanging out at some party."

"Umm no, this picture I am looking at has Dontay sticking his tongue down your throat!!"

"WHAT? NO WAY!!"

"Why would I lie? I am about to screenshot it and send it to you." "Amara I don't know where that picture came from, I have never kissed Dontay. I have never even been interested in him." While Taj was talking, Amara was taking a picture of her screen to send Taj the picture that she knew nothing about. Amara was so frustrated and tired of the drama that just kept attaching itself to Dontay. She sat thinking to herself that he wasn't even worth it, and it was time to separate herself from everyone except Lysa and

Lace. "OMG! Amara I swear we never took this picture, this never happened." "Oh now you're such a celebrity that people are manipulating your pictures? Yeah right. You're not even famous, you're parents are. You're a nobody who just lost another friend!" "Amara that is really low and cruel. But hey you're entitled to your opinions. Glad I know how you really feel. Goodbye." After Taj ended the call, Amara set up on her bed and just stared at the picture. She couldn't believe it.

CHAPTER TWENTY

Over the next few days, Amara did a good job of avoiding Taj and Dontay. Even though Mrs. Loy had a class during Amara's lunch period, she agreed to let Amara sit in her classroom. Sitting in the classroom during lunch, allowed Amara to get a head start on her homework. Amara was excited about that, because it allowed her extra time to play with DJ.

Lace and Sky had been calling constantly, and Amara was set on ignoring them both. The only person she was talking to was Lysa. They had made plans for Amara to come over the upcoming weekend to spend the night, and Amara could hardly wait.

DJ was sitting on Amara's bed with all his attention locked into the movie *Cars*. Amara was watching the movie with DJ, but had started dozing off when a notification alert rang out from her phone. She got up off her bed and walked over to get her phone out of her purse.

Unlocking the screen, she was shocked to see that she had a DM (direct message) on Instagram. Amara hardly ever got private messages on Instagram. When she opened the message it was a picture of a flyer for a party. The message read *"We want you here!!"* Amara was puzzled because she did not know the person who sent her the message.

When she went to the person's profile, there was no picture and it was private so she couldn't see any pictures. She called

Lysa to see what she should do. Lysa was always down to go party, so she said they should go and check it out. They stayed on the phone until Lysa heard her dad calling her.

Amara was trying to really stay off of social media, because she got more and more upset whenever she saw pictures of Dontay. He had been sending text messages and constantly calling, but she refused to respond. He had even asked her grandmother to try to talk to her, but Amara was over him. She just wished that everyone would stop trying, and let her breathe.

She couldn't resist it any more so she opened Instagram back up and went to Dontay's profile and started scrolling. Completely losing track of time, she must have been scrolling for a long time because when she finally spotted another picture it was from 77 weeks ago. Of course, it was another picture of him and some girl. The longer she looked at the picture, the more she started to recognize the girl's face. It was one of the girls that had jumped on her at the school.

Amara was definitely done with Dontay now. She couldn't believe that he was such a big liar. He had everyone fooled, especially her grandmother! Well no more for Amara. She was leaving him alone, and was even more excited about spending the weekend with Lysa.

***

"Hey Amara, did you ever think you would be doing such grown up stuff at only twelve?" Lysa asked while they were sitting in the room watching *Teen Mom* on MTV.

"No! Most times I ask myself what I'm doing. Sometimes it is not even fun. We aren't acting like adults if we have to sneak around."

"Yeah sometimes it is not fun, but you do know that adults are sneaky too right?"

"Of course, don't you remember Dwayne?"

Amara zoned out and started daydreaming. She wondered how her life would be if her mom and Dwayne were still married. In her short twelve years of being on the earth, she had seen and experienced a lot. After what her mother went through with Dwayne, Dontay being a liar, and even the stories she had heard about her father, she was beginning to think that guys were nothing more than bad headaches.

"So do you still want to go to the party tonight?"

Amara was still so deep in thought; she didn't hear Lysa talking to her.

"Earth to Amara, HELLO!"

"Huh?" Amara asked finally hearing Lysa talking to her.

"I asked do you still want to go the party? You sound like your starting to feel guilty." "Not guilty, just trying to figure out what is making me act like this all of the sudden. I never was defiant towards my mom and grandma." "Yeah I do remember you being an angel when we were little. Everyone else was getting popped and you were always somewhere with your grandmother." "I know right! I hated to get in trouble, and if my grandma popped me, I felt like my world was coming to an end. Now I just don't even care. Everyone adult in my life is making their own decisions not caring about how I feel, so I'm only worried about me from now on. So now about this party!" The girls spent the rest of the evening planning what they were going to wear the next night to the party. Amara was getting that feeling again telling her that going to the party would be a bad idea. Like every other time, she ignored the feeling and was determined to go to the party.

CHAPTER TWENTY-ONE

This party started earlier than normal, so the girls didn't have to sneak out. They just lied about how they would be getting home. The plans were to just go and see who was there, and who had sent Amara the flyer. Well you know what they say about plans!

"Hey Amara!"

"Sky...did you send me the flyer?"

"Flyer? No, I was just about to ask you how did you know about this party?"

Amara was confused, but before she could ask any more questions she saw the girl from the picture that had also been a part of jumping on her. The girl walked over to Sky and whispered something in her ear before walking away.

"What was that all about?"

"Oh she was telling me that one of the guests was on their way."

"Sky, are you really about to sit here and act like you don't know who that girl is? What is her name?"

"Sade? Yes I know her. What is wrong with you?"

THE SEARCH FOR AMARA

Amara and Lysa shared a quick look. Lysa didn't know exactly what was going on, but she could tell by the look on Amara's face that something was not right.

"Sky, Sade was one of the girls that jumped me at the school!"

"Oh, how was I supposed to know that?"

"Wow, never mind. I will see you later."

"Wait, Amara don't leave."

"There is no reason for me to be here. I don't know what is going on. I know that she recognized me, and I don't even know who invited me."

"Please! Just stay Amara, please!"

"Ok I will stay for another thirty minutes, and then we have to leave."

Sky knew that she was going to have to move quickly. Of course Sade recognized Amara; it was her that had sent the message. The girls were still out to get revenge about Dontay. They didn't care that Amara wasn't with him; they just wanted her out of the picture.

Lysa looked across the yard and saw Mario holding a beer bottle in his hands. She immediately started sweating. With this crowd, he was sure to find out that she was not seventeen. She tried to move out of his view, but it was too late. Mario was walking towards her with a huge smile on his face.

"Lysa here comes your little boyfriend," Amara said in a sing song voice.

Amara laughter came to quick stop, when she noticed that Lysa looked horrified. She looked like she was going to faint at any moment.

"Lysa are you ok?"

Before she could answer though Mario was standing in front of them.

"Hey Lysa, I didn't think I would see you tonight."

"Oh."

"Why you looking like you saw a ghost?"

"I didn't expect to see you here tonight either...ummm...what are you doing here?"

"Just about everyone here got a flyer invite and we are trying to figure out who invited us."

"Everyone? How many people are here?"

"About 25."

"That's it?"

"Yeah, that's enough! How about we go somewhere and talk."

Lysa wasn't sure about going off with Mario alone, especially since she hadn't talked to him since the last time she saw him. Before she could agree or disagree Mario took her hand, and started pulling her into another room.

Amara wanted to say something, but Mario was looking determined and Lysa was not pulling away so she kept quiet. Now she was standing there looking around, because she didn't recognize the other people standing around.

"Amara, girl what is she doing here?"

Amara whipped around to see Taj pointing towards her, while talking to Sky. Sky pulled her quickly out the room. Amara was starting to feel uncomfortable. Taj, Sky, and one of the girls that had jumped on her were all here. Lysa had went off somewhere with Mario, so she was really by herself.

Looking around trying to find somewhere to sit until Lysa reappeared, she saw a chair in the back out the way. She quickly walked that way, hoping that she could get over there unnoticed.

Amara pulled out her phone to occupy the time, she was really starting to wish she had listen to that strange feeling and just stayed at Lysa's house. Movement caught her eye and she looked up just in time to see Dontay walking into the party. She started to get up, but decided at the last minute to sit back and see what happens.

Taj came out from the back or wherever she was and walked up to Dontay, putting her arms around his neck. Amara started getting angry and hot. Dontay just stood still. He didn't hug Taj back, but he didn't push away either.

Sky walked up behind Amara, "I told you not to trust her."

Amara couldn't believe it and she couldn't take anymore, she got out of the chair and ran outside. She knew she would be in trouble, but she had to get away from the party so she called her grandmother. After what seemed like a million questions, Alicia told Amara she was on her way to get her.

***

"Amara, what were you doing on this side of town? Where does your mother think you are? How did you even get over here?"

Amara burst out in tears. Reality hit her hard. She was only twelve years old, what was she doing?

"Girl dry up those tears, it is time to have a heart to heart. This behavior is unacceptable."

Amara knew that her grandmother was going to let her have it, and if she called her mother Amara's life was over. She would never see freedom again. Her mother would probably try to figure out a way to homeschool her. She was really sorry for her actions, but she knew nobody wanted to hear that.

Alicia was ranting and raving the whole ride, but Amara had tuned her out and was praying for God to save her life. Finally they pulled up to the house. Amara's heart almost stopped beating when she saw her mother and Lysa's father standing outside with scowls on their face.

She wished that she could just disappear. In the midst of everything that was going on, she had forgotten about Lysa. How was she going to explain to Lysa's dad what was going on? Amara had got herself into a world of trouble, and now she had included her friend in it also.

"Don't delay the consequences. Get out of the car."

"Amara get your ass over here right now! What the hell is wrong with you? Where were you? Where is Lysa? Are you crazy?"

Amara never understood why adults would always ask a bunch of questions back to back. How was she supposed to answer? Did they want the questions answered in the order they were asked? She was trying to find the words to say.

"Amara, I just need to know where my daughter is. Was she with you? Did you leave her?

Great now it was time for Mr. Payne to fire off his round of questions. Before Amara could respond, her phone started ringing. She tried to silence it, but Asha walked over and snatched it out of her pocket.

"Dontay, Amara will not be answering this phone anymore for a very long time!"

"Asha, can you ask him if Lysa is wherever he is at?"

"Dontay did you hear Mr. Payne...she just left? With who? WHAT!! Ok, ok, do you have their number? Text it to Amara's phone. Thanks!"

Asha turned to Mr. Payne and shared the information that Dontay had just given her. Lysa had been at the party, but she had just left with some guy. Dontay swore that he tried to stop her, but Lysa was drunk and yelling at him. He said that the guy who was older said he would take good care of her, and would make sure she got back home safe.

Mr. Payne was trying his best not to breakdown into tears. All types of horror stories started running through his mind. Was his precious daughter going to be part of sex trafficking, rape, was she being drugged? He couldn't it in anymore.

"LORD JESUS!!!! Amara what were you girls thinking, do you not understand the dangers?"

"I am so sorry, we were just having fun. We didn't think that something like this would happen."

"Right! YOU DID NOT THINK!" Asha was pissed and worried all at the same time.

Finally the notification came through Amara's phone creating a distraction, and removing the attention off of her, even if only for a brief moment. It didn't last long at all.

"Amara call this little boy. Better yet, what were we thinking? Call Lysa, now!"

Shaking with terror, Amara reached out and took her phone. She dialed Lysa's phone. It went unanswered just like Amara knew it would. Looking up at her mother, she immediately put her head back down and went to her text messages to get the number so she could call Mario next.

"Yo, who dis?"

Amara was shocked; Mario didn't look like he had a hood demeanor.

"Umm, is this Mario?"

"Yeah, who dis?"

"This is Amara, is my friend Lysa with you?"

"Yeah baby girl she is good hands, I put her to sleep. You feel me?"

Amara tried not to let her facial expressions give anything away. Mario was yelling, so she prayed no one could hear him. Asha threw that prayer right out the window when she mouthed to Amara to put the phone on speaker.

She was terrified what was going to come out of Mario's mouth, now that everyone could hear him.

"Mario, I really need to speak with Lysa please."

"Didn't I just tell you that she is sleeping? I will have her call you tomorrow."

"Listen here you asshole, this is Lysa's father."

"Hey, sorry I couldn't meet you under different circumstances. Why all the name calling?"

"Prick, how old are you?"

"Dude, stop calling me out of my name or I'm going to have to end the call."

"Nineteen"

"NINETEEN!!!! Do you know how old Lysa is?"

"Of course, she is seventeen," Mario answered matter of factly.

"No she is not, she is fourteen."

"Awww damn G, she lied to me. LYSA, LYSA, wake yo ass up!!"

"Stop yelling at my daughter."

Mario disconnected the call, and chaos broke out. Lysa's dad started screaming and shaking Amara, which led to Asha punching his back, but her hits were not fazing him. Henry came outside and fired a warning shot into the air.

"What the hell is going on out here?"

Alicia ran over to her husband. While pushing him back into the house, she was explaining what was going on. She explained the anger that Mr. Payne was showing was actually just fear because his fourteen year old daughter was out with some nineteen year old thug.

Henry was ready to go outside and smack Amara himself. He could not believe all this trouble his granddaughter had caused. Everyone came in before he could go out, and Amara went running up the stairs with Asha hot on her trail. The night was just the beginning of a nightmare.

CHAPTER TWENTY-TWO

The sun was appearing on the horizon, and no one had gotten any sleep. They still had no idea where Lysa was, and Mario had either turned his phone off or the battery had died. Mr. Payne had called the police, but they told him he could file a report until she had been missing for twenty-four hours. Lysa's mom had been calling the house every hour on the hour to see if anything had changed.

Alicia had called for Pastor Rob to come over. Asha had finally had enough and just walked out. They were all just sitting around the table worrying and wondering about what would happen next. Amara's phone had been buzzing nonstop. She was scared to turn it off in case Lysa tried to call her.

"Amara come with me upstairs so we can talk."

Amara pushed back from the table and slowly walked across the kitchen. She felt she was walking to her death sentence. The feeling of the unknown was driving her insane. They still hadn't heard anything from Lysa, her mother had just left without saying a word, and now her grandmother wanted to talk to her.

Slowly she approached her room trying to control her breathing so that she didn't pass out.

"Come in and sit down Amara. I need to share some things with you before Pastor gets here."

Amara decided to take a seat on the floor. She sat, crossed her legs Indian style, and leaned up against the wall. The first words out of her mother's voice shocked her so much; she had to quickly cover her to mouth to stop from screaming out.

Alicia was explaining to Amara that the phase of life she was going through was normal, but it would be better if she learned early and stopped before she went too far. Lysa's disappearance was a lesson of what could happen. She should use this lesson to get it together before something happened to her.

Amara listened to everything that her grandmother was telling her, but what could she really say? Adults always want to share their stories of how they did the same things when you they were the same age. Their stories were interesting, but times were always changing. It was impossible for Amara's grandmother to understand. Alicia couldn't have even done some of things kids Amara's age were doing now, they didn't have technology like this back in her day.

Voices started getting extremely loud. Alicia got up and made it across the room to the door with amazing speed. She and Amara both went running down the stairs. They entered the kitchen to Mr. Payne choking Dontay, and everyone trying to get Mr. Payne's hands off of his neck.

Alicia ran over and smacked Mr. Payne in the back of his head.

"Sir, you will not do that in my house. What are you mad at this young man for anyway?"

"He knows where my daughter is!"

"Momma Alicia, I promise I do not know where Lysa is at. I don't know anyone who hangs with Mario. I have been trying to find out all night if anyone knows where he lives."

"Dontay I know you would tell us or even take us to Lysa if you knew where she was at. You don't have to explain to me."

"Wait, Dontay how old are you?"

"Payne, where are you going with your questions?" Henry asked.

"I'm sitting here trying to understand why this young man is so comfortable coming around like he is family. I know that he likes Amara, but isn't she only twelve?"

"Listen Mr. Payne, we understand your pain and frustration with your daughter being missing. However do not take the frustration out on the people that are here to help you," Alicia said with sadness in her tone.

"You are right. I apologize to everyone. I think I am going to go home with my wife, I know you all will contact me if you hear anything. Amara I truly hope you take this as a learning experience. Goodbye everyone, again I apologize for my outburst."

Everyone just looked around at each other. No one knew what to say. Henry walked out of the kitchen. He was furious that his

Amara, who could do no wrong in his eyes was involved such a scary situation. All his wife wanted to do was pray, but he wanted to take his search to the streets.

The doorbell rang, and Henry went to his room instead of going to the door. He knew that Pastor Rob was at the door, and he was not in the mood to hear a sermon. Alicia went to the door and invited Pastor Rob into the den. Dontay came in and shook hands with Pastor Rob before sitting on the couch.

"Amara, Pastor Rob is here!" Alicia called out to the kitchen.

Amara just wanted the night to be over with. She had been praying all day that Lysa would just get dropped off at home, they would get their punishment and life could start going back to normal. Before her grandmother could call her again, she got up and went into the den. She was prepared for Pastor Rob to lecture her.

"Amara, honey I am so sorry that you are going through such a trying time. Why don't you come on and let us talk about what is going on."

Amara really wasn't in the mood to talk. She was really hoping that they would just lecture and preach, and she could she just listen. Knowing that no matter what she said, they would not understand or believe her, so talking was a waste of time.

"Let's all bow our heads first and say a prayer."

***

THE SEARCH FOR AMARA

Pastor Rob finally left and Amara went up to her room. She had left Dontay downstairs with her grandmother. He was persistent to try to get Amara talk about what had happened the night before. She didn't want to talk about anything. All she wanted to do was go to sleep and hopefully wake up to find it was just a bad dream.

An alert went off on her phone. It was a siren that she had never heard before. She started to ignore it, but it just kept going and going. When she picked up her phone, she dropped it and started screaming.

Alicia and Henry got up the stairs in record time. Henry opened the door to find Amara on the floor still screaming and crying. Alicia walked over to her and bent down next to her.

"Honey what is the matter?" Amara could not breathe, "Grandma..Ly..Ly..Lysa..LYSAA."

"Lysa what? What is it? What?"

Amara fell back on the floor, she knew that Lysa was with Mario somewhere but getting an Amber Alert made it a reality that her friend was really missing.

Henry picked up Amara's phone and figured out what had his granddaughter in hysterics.

"Alicia, Mr. Payne got the authorities to issue an Amber Alert for Lysa."

Alicia quickly glanced up and then pulled in Amara tight for a hug. She knew that her granddaughter was terrified. At first it was just girls sneaking out, and her friend not coming home. Now it was really serious, because everyone would know that Lysa was missing.

Hearing footsteps coming up the stairs reminded everyone that Dontay was still in the house. He knocked on the door, and everyone said come in. He nervously pushed open the door, and knew that Amara must have already got the alert.

Dontay wanted to go and hug Amara, but instead he just stood in the door. Silence once again overtook everyone. The house phone ringing downstairs was just going to go unanswered because they were all frozen in their thoughts of what if and what now.

Amara's body must have finally given up on her. She was lightly snoring, and her grandfather picked up her off the floor and placed her in her bed. Alicia grabbed Dontay's hand and they exited the room to go downstairs.

Dontay figured it would be best for him to go home, but before he left Henry asked a lot of questions about Mario. Most of the questions Dontay couldn't answer though. He wished he had at least some good guesses because he wanted Lysa back home just like everyone else.

CHAPTER TWENTY-THREE

Another day went by with no news about Lysa. It was Sunday and Amara was expected to get up and go to church. She just laid in bed, and wondered where God was in the midst of all this. She thought the God would never let harm come near them since they were saved. Amara was upset with God, and she didn't want to go to church.

She planned on faking a stomach ache when her grandmother came upstairs. Hopefully she could stay home with her grandfather. Pastor Rob had been so determined to preach about how the Bible instructed her to honor and obey. Well what about His promises never to leave nor forsake? He had let her friend stay missing with no contact for twenty-four whole hours, and counting.

A soft knock on her door prompted her to turn towards the wall. It would be easier to pretend that she was sick if she didn't have to face her grandmother.

"Amara, honey are you up?"

Amara laid still and thought that maybe if she didn't answer, she would be left alone.

"Amara...ok I will let you rest. Your grandfather was going to go church with me this morning, but I will let him know you are not up to going. I know that you are not sleep though. I will let you stay home this time, and I will send up prayers for you and Lysa."

She couldn't figure out how her grandmother always knew exactly what was going on. She was surprised that her grandmother didn't know that her and her friends have been sneaking out of the house. Laying still staring at the wall for about fifteen minutes had her on her way back to sleep.

The vibration from her phone made Amara almost jump out the bed. Feeling around with her eyes still closed, she got frustrated because she couldn't find her phone before it stopped ringing. As soon as she fell back asleep, it started vibrating again. This time she opened her eyes and found her phone all the way at the end of the bed.

"Hello."

"Amara you have to wake up, I need you to get Dontay to come get me."

"LYSA?"

"Yes, look I will answer all of your questions when you get here. I'm going to text you the street names that I see, and then I have to go hide so no one will see me. I have to go before my phone dies. I will text you; please don't let anyone but Dontay know that you have talked to me."

Before Amara could respond Lysa had ended the call. She jumped up to throw on some clothes, praying that Dontay had not gone to church either.

"Hey!"

"Dontay meet me at the corner in three minutes."

"Huh?"

"Just be there please."

Now Amara had to figure out how she was going to get past her grandfather. Hopefully he was still sleeping. She pulled her jogging pants up over her pajama pants, and grabbed her hoodie. Creeping to the top of the stairs, she listened first for any stirring around downstairs.

She didn't hear anything so she tiptoed down the stairs, and took off her shoes when she got to the bottom of the stairs that her footsteps wouldn't be heard walking across the floor. When she got to the door she made a break for it.

When she got to the corner, Dontay was sitting there waiting for her. She checked her phone; she saw that Lysa had sent her a text. She opened it and read the streets off to Dontay telling him to drive. She wasn't familiar with the area, but she noticed that Dontay was looking at her sort of weird.

"So are you ready to talk?"

"No I am not ready to talk."

"Well can you at least tell me where we are going?"

Amara blew her breath out in a long sigh full of frustration, "You will find out when we get there, please just drive."

"I will stop this car and put it in park if you do not tell me why we are going into such a dangerous neighborhood."

"Dontay please just drive. It is very important that we get there."

Dontay had a feeling that they were going to get Lysa, but he just wanted to hear Amara say it. He turned the music back up, and just drove. Amara's birthday was coming up, but after this latest incident he highly doubted that if her mother would let her do anything or go anywhere.

The car was stopped at a red light when they saw Lysa running towards them at top speed. Dontay hit the unlock button, and Amara sat in shock. She felt like she was in a movie. Lysa jumped in the backseat just as the light turned green. She grabbed Amara from the back and just started sobbing uncontrollably.

Dontay didn't know what to do so he pulled into the first gas station that they came to and put the car in the park. Lysa and Amara both couldn't stop crying. They had got out the car and were just hugging each other and sobbing. They were starting to attract unwanted attention, and Dontay was not quite sure how to handle two girls crying.

Dontay's phone started ringing. He recognized the number and told the girls to hurry up and get back in the car. He made sure they were in and the pulled off, before he answered the phone.

"Hello"

"Tay man, you talk to Lysa?"

"Naw, but her pops is looking for her. I thought she was with you."

"She was with me, but when I came back she was gone."

Mario had no idea that an Amber Alert had been issued and that he was listed as the last person seen with Lysa with a description of his car. He had disabled the alert a long time ago when it woke him up out of his sleep for a little girl missing from a city he had never even heard of.

"Uh-oh, did you call her phone?"

The girls were looking back and forth between each other and then back to Dontay. Lysa was shaking with fear. She hadn't got a chance to tell Amara any details yet, but it was obvious something terrible had happened.

"Yeah, but it is going straight to voicemail. Ok if you talk to her tell her to call me."

"Ok but if she is back home, none of us will probably be talking to her anytime soon."

"Yeah, I hear you. Alright man, holla."

Lysa fell back with a sigh of relief. She was not ready to go home and face her parents, but she was so happy that she was away from Mario. She put her head back and tried to get some sleep on the drive home.

Dontay kept glancing at Amara. He decided that it would be best to just keep her as friend or even a little sister. She was not as mature as he originally thought. This sneaking out and leaving her friend at a party really showed him a side of her that reminded him just how young she was.

The crazy part was that Dontay didn't even know that he was the reason that Amara had left the party in such a rush. He still had no clue that she had saw him and Taj. He pulled up to Lysa's house. Amara was scared for her friend. Lysa knew that he parents were going to be very angry with her, but she didn't know the extremes that they had went through. She hugged Amara, popped Dontay upside the head and was out the car. Her parents came flying out the house. Mr. Payne was yelling at her while her mother was crying and hugging her, thanking God that she was back home safe. Lysa didn't know what to do, so she just held her mother and released even more tears after she heard her father calling to cancel the Amber Alert.

CHAPTER TWENTY-FOUR

Asha had pulled another disappearing act and still had not returned ever since that day she left Alicia's house. The only difference was this time she had DJ with her, because Delilah said he was not there with her. Henry was upset beyond words this time. Amara needed her mother; Asha being gone was not setting a good example.

Amara had gone back to school and was getting back into her regular routine. However she had cut everyone off. She had absolutely zero friends, and her grandparents made her turn in her phone and tablet as soon as she walked through the door. She was allowed to only do homework while monitored in the kitchen. No electronics were allowed in her room.

The one good thing about the punishment was that it had brought back her love for reading. Taj was back trying to cause her problems at school. Rumors were spreading that Taj and Dontay were a couple. Whenever Amara would see them at school she would go the other way.

Lace had been trying to get in contact with her, but she was actually enjoying her alone time without any distractions. She was missing her little brother like crazy though. Asha was not answering her phone this time for anybody, and Amara was starting to wonder if she had left this time for good.

Alicia had come in the kitchen one day while Amara was doing homework and told her that Mr. Payne had called to inform them that they were sending Lysa out of town to live with relatives. Amara felt so bad for her, because she knew that Lysa was devastated to go live with people she didn't even know.

Sky was back being Amara's shadow, but it only worked at school. It was impossible to talk to her outside of school with everything taken away from her. Her grandparents did not play when it came to punishments. This was another reason she wished that her mother would hurry up and come back.

Asha never did enforce strong and lasting punishments. She would take something and give it back before the day was over. Amara was starting to feel horrible, she felt like her mother was not going to come back this time for good.

Even though Amara had formed a routine of school, home, read, sleep, start over, she was getting bored and restless. She started thinking would could possibly happen to her if she got into any more trouble.

The next day at school she overheard Sky telling a group of girls about an upcoming party the following weekend. Amara knew it would be impossible for her to go. If she even thought about sneaking out of her grandparent's house, they would kill her.

"Amara are you coming?" Sky asked.

"Sky now you know that I can't even get out of the house to go somewhere to sneak out."

"Dang girl, you really still on punishment?"

"Yes my grandma is nothing like my mother. If she puts you on punishment, oh you are so on punishment until whenever she decided you have learned your lesson!"

"Don't they go to sleep early?"

Amara's conscience was trying to warn her to not even linger on the thought. Why was she even considering doing anything with Sky? She had already proven several times that she could not be trusted.

"No, I'm not doing it."

"Well, ok! This is the last party before the summer. You will be sad you missed it."

Amara doubted it, but it was just something she would have to miss out on. However before she could respond Taj came over and flopped down at the table. She stared at Amara in silence for what felt like ten minutes.

"Is there problem?" Amara asked.

"Yeah actually there is, I am trying to figure out how your young ass has my man hooked on you. Did you have sex with him?"

Oh boy, Amara thought. She was not in the mood for this foolishness again. She started cleaning up her things at the table so she could dismiss herself. When she went to stand up, Taj pushed her back down.

"Taj do not put your hands on me again."

"Well then sit down and answer my question little girl."

Amara was fuming. She hated when someone called her a little girl. Taking deep breaths to calm her down, once again she started to stand up. This time Taj jumped up and pushed her down on the floor. That was the final straw.

Amara had made a promise to herself when those girls jumped her that she would never be on the losing end of a fight again. Before Taj could do anything else, Amara jumped up and snatched the lunch tray off the table.

She began beating Taj over the head with the tray over and over again. She was swinging the tray so hard and so wild that the tray was hitting Taj all over her body. Amara heard the alarm ring to alert security that there was a fight going on.

Knowing that they were on their way to break up the fight and feeling like now she had a point to prove, Amara took the tray and hit Taj two good times in the face before dropping it on the floor. Amara was so full of rage that she had actually blacked out while fighting.

When security entered into the cafeteria and grabbed her, she noticed that Taj was covered in blood. However Amara didn't feel any remorse. Staring at her, she wished she could do more. The kids that had been so loud and rowdy during the fight were now dead silent.

Taj was lying out on the floor. She said she couldn't walk and she kept yelling out that she couldn't feel her face. Amara heard one of the security guards say into his walkie talkie that 911 needed to be called.

Before Amara could fully process what was happening she was snatched up and drug out of the cafeteria down to the principal's office. Security started explaining that a phone call needed to be made to her parents. Due to the fact that she had used what was considered a weapon and 911 had to be called for Taj, the police would be taking Amara down to Juvenile Justice.

Amara couldn't believe that once again her world was spinning out of control. When Mrs. Hollow called her grandmother, she put her on speaker phone. To say that Alicia was pissed was an understatement. The breaking point for Amara was when her grandmother said she would not be down to get her and disconnected the call.

Mrs. Hollow looked at Amara with disappointment and disgust. She could not believe that the girl that was sitting in front of her was the same girl that was described in the file in front of her.

"What happened out there?"

Amara just sat staring at the wall, she refused to answer. She was once again in a situation where the adult would not believe her or understand what was going on.

"Amara, I am here to help you. I can't help, if I don't know what's going on."

She still set there refusing to speak.

"Ok well suit yourself; the officers will be here soon. Hopefully you can settle this matter without serious consequences such as jail time."

Right after Mrs. Hollow said that, there was a knock on the door and when she said come in, two female police officers entered. The twelve almost thirteen year old innocence and fear took over Amara. Was she really about to be locked up? Where they really going to place her in handcuffs and make her ride in the back of a police car?

All of her questions were answered when the officer told her to stand up, turn around and place her arms behind her back. One officer started issuing her Miranda rights, while the other officer was explaining to Mrs. Hollow what had happened based on the statements she had received from the students. Too much was going on and Amara couldn't take it, so she snapped. "NOOOOOOO, I can't go to jail! I was defending myself. Why is this happening to me? I want my mommy. Can you please call my mommy? PLEASE!" Almost everyone in the room felt sorry for Amara, but procedures were procedures, and they had to do their jobs. Mrs. Hollow did promise to call Asha, while trying to calm her down. The officer who was putting the handcuffs on her felt no remorse. She felt like the kids in this school were stuck up and needed to be taught some lessons. Mrs. Hollow requested that they take Amara out the back way, so she would not have to walk the halls for everyone to see her. The officer with the chip on her shoulder smacked her lips. This was what she meant. She felt like walking the hall would embarrass and maybe prevent this type of behavior from happening again. Her partner had seniority though, so she had to follow what she wanted done. Amara dragged her feet while being pulled towards the door. She couldn't believe that she was really about to be riding in the back of a police car like a criminal. When she got outside, she held her head down in shame. Even though she had gone out the back, it was still a crowd of students watching her as she walked to the police car. She looked up just in time to see the stretcher with Taj on it being lifted into the back of the ambulance. This day would go down as one of the most humiliating days of her life.

Chapter Twenty-Five

Amara luckily did not have to go through the whole process. When authorities took her before the probation officer who had the authority to go forward or release her, she was released based on the witness statements that proved Amara was only defending herself.

Asha was there waiting on her daughter. She could not believe the call she got from her mother, especially when Alicia told her that she absolutely refused to go get Amara. Asha really had to get herself together so that she could be the mother that she was supposed to be. In less than a month, her daughter had gotten caught sneaking out to go to a party, her friend had been missing, and now she had been arrested.

After about three hours of waiting, Amara was escorted out to the waiting area where she ran and fell into her mother's arms sobbing.

"Mommy, I am so sorry. I didn't mean to get locked up. I was just defending myself. Taj pushed me on the floor, because she is mad about Dontay. I don't want Dontay. I don't want a boyfriend anymore; I just want to go back to hanging out and having fun with Lace and being a teenager."

Those words were like music to Asha's ears. It was in this moment that Asha realized that even though her daughter was smart and mature, she was still just a little girl. Asha had totally taken her focus off of being a mother trying to keep up with Dwayne and his doings. She was driving herself crazy following and spying on him and Melissa.

It was time to move on and focus on her children. She grabbed Amara tight, kissed the top of her head and promised her that everything was going to be alright.

***

Even though it had been proven that Amara was defending herself, because of the severity of the fight the school still had to issue a ten day suspension. Amara also had to go before the school board and prove that she knew how to conduct herself in the future, if a situation like this was to occur again.

Taj however would not be returning. Not because of the school's decision, but because her pride would not allow her to show her face again.

Amara had celebrated her thirteenth birthday would the minimum of a simple store bought birthday cake with her mother, grandparents, DJ, Delilah, Lace, and Mariah.

Lace and Amara had started building their friendship back. Delilah had been around more and more being a friend to Asha. Amara still didn't like or trust her, but her mother was not leaving for weeks at a time and she was finally starting to seem happy again.

Alicia was still so upset with her granddaughter that she was not speaking to her. Amara had explained to her grandfather everything that had happened. He was proud of his granddaughter for standing up for herself, but he did tell her that she had gone a little too far.

Asha knew that making mistakes was a huge part of growing up, and that is why she was not so harsh with punishments. Although the only place Amara was allowed to stay the night, was over to Delilah's with Lace.

With Taj gone, and Amara creating a reputation to not be messed with Sky was only hanging around her and she was sure to keep her mouth closed and not start stuff or spread lies. Amara really was a true friend and Sky was determined to not mess up again.

The school year was coming to an end, and Asha had let Amara once again get some privileges back again. Alicia was so mad, she felt like Amara would never learn lessons because she never suffered any major consequences.

Amara was spending the weekend with Sky. She had called her grandmother and asked could she come get them Sunday morning and take them to church. Alicia told her no. Amara was heartbroken. What happened to her Bible quoting grandmother that always preached to her about forgiveness?

Sky had been talking to this boy name Jonathan on Kik for a few weeks. She couldn't even remember how they had met, but he had been begging her to come over. She was terrified to go by herself, but today she would have Amara around. She knew that

THE SEARCH FOR AMARA

Amara had been staying out of trouble, but it was harmless to meet some friends at a park.

Sky sent Jonathan a message and asked him did he have a friend and could they meet at the park tonight. Jonathan immediately replied that his brother Kevin could come with him, and that they were planning to go to a party at a friend's house. Jonathan was sixteen, and Kevin was fifteen. Sky replied that was cool, they could meet at the park and walk to the party together.

When Sky told Amara the plans she agreed. It sounded like just regular teen fun. As it started getting later and later, Amara questioned if they were still going to the park. Sky admitted that she forgot to leave out the detail of going once it got dark.

"Sky what is really going on? Why are we meeting at the park at night?"

"Ok Amara, Jonathan and his brother invited us to a party. We are going to meet at the park and walk to the party together."

"Sky, why would you trick me?"

"I'm sorry. I just really want to see Jonathan in person, but I have been scared to meet him by myself. I knew if I just mentioned the party you would say no."

"Maybe, maybe not. Well I hope his brother is cute at least."

"Girl I hope Jonathan is cute!"

"Wait you have never seen him at all?"

"No he keeps saying he wants me to get to know him as a person, and not just like him because of his looks."

"Sky that does not sound like something a sixteen year old would say. I'm not sure about this."

"He says a lot of things sixteen year olds WE are used to would not say."

"What does that mean, WE?"

"They are white Amara!"

"WHAT"

"Yep, we are about to go meet some white boys."

While Sky could not stop laughing, Amara was not entertained. She had nothing against white people. Last year the majority of her classmates were white, but she just never thought about liking a white boy as anything more than a friend.

"Sky you are crazy and now I am even more scared. Wait a minute, if you have never seen him, how do you know he is white?"

"He has to be! Why else would he not want to me to know what he looks like?"

"You are really stupid. So you THINK they are white, but you don't know? Maybe he doesn't want you to know what he looks like because he is ugly. Did that thought cross your mind?"

"Yeah it did, but I talked to him on the phone and he sounds like a white boy."

"What does a white boy sound like Sky?"

"You know like Nick Jonas."

THE SEARCH FOR AMARA

Amara doubled over with laughter. She could not believe the logic that was running through Sky's head right now. How did Amara get herself in the middle of this craziness? Well this time around it would not be sneaking out, because Sky's mother was already gone.

Asha had met Sky's parents in the past, but what she didn't know was that they were getting a divorce and now Sky's mom was working at night because she had to get two jobs to afford to stay in the house she was in. The girls were under no supervision.

Sky walked into her closet to try to find something cute enough to wear to the party, but comfortable enough to walk to the park in. Amara had suggested that she just wear a cute shirt and some jeans. Sky refused, saying that she didn't want to show up to the park looking like twins.

Amara thought wearing anything more would be crazy and a waste of time. She put her clothes across the bed and tuned back into to one of her favorite shows that she had started watching on On Demand. Amara had fallen asleep and didn't even realize it until she heard Sky screaming her name. Opening her eyes and seeing how dark it was outside, her first thought was maybe Sky had changed her mind about meeting Jonathan and Kevin. "Amara get up, girl I thought you were dressed already! Let's go, the guys have already left out." Amara got up slowly. She still had the feeling that this was not a good idea. She tried to talk Sky out of again while sliding into her jeans. It proved to be a waste of time.

Sky was determined. "Amara look I am going with or without you." "Sky I am just telling you how I am feeling. Every time I get this feeling, something bad always happens." "Well don't go, like I said." "Sky cut it out, I am not going to let you go meet some guys you know nothing about by yourself. Just remember that I told you before we went that I have a bad feeling." "What happened to speaking positive words and thinking positive thoughts?" "You right. Ok I am ready," Amara responded while pulling her shirt down over her head. "You ready finally?" "Yeah, are you?" Sky was still applying makeup, and the curlers were still plugged up. She took a final look in the mirror, unplugged the curlers and got ready to walk out of the bathroom. "Wait, Amara! You are not going to put on any makeup?" "Girl no, it is dark outside! Who is going to be paying attention to my face?" "At least put some eyeshadow or something." "No I am not; I will put on my usual lip gloss. Now let's GO!"

CHAPTER TWENTY-SIX

Alicia's spirit could not rest. She knew that something was wrong with somebody close to her. Tears were pouring from her eyes and all she knew to do was to call out,

"JESUS, JESUS, JESUS, JESUS!"

She was being too stubborn to call Asha to check on her and Amara; she just prayed that God would keep them safe from all dangers and harm. Amara had no idea that her grandmother's prayers stopped the weapon that had formed already, from being able to prosper.

When they got to the park, they had walked right past the guys at first. Sky sent Jonathan a message asking *where were they at?* He immediately replied for her to turn around and walk back. Sky read the message, and Amara started shaking. They had only walked past some dudes that looked like they were nowhere near fifteen and sixteen.

The guy that must be Jonathan walked over to Sky and grabbed her aggressively. He had to be well over six feet, and upon closer inspection they were young. They were just big like football players and Sky was right, they were white.

"You must be Amara, oh my goodness you are beautiful. I am Kevin."

Amara was so focused on Jonathan and Sky that she hadn't even heard him walk up to her. She had to admit he was nice looking. Kevin was tall and cocky like his brother but he had a sweet innocence to himself. At least that is what Amara assumed. Little did she and Sky know but they were about to walk into a world that they knew nothing about.

They all started walking towards a hotel that was down the street. That was where the party was being held. Kevin pulled some gummi bears out of his pocket and asked Amara did she want some. Of course she accepted and started munching. The first one had a bit of an odd taste to it, but she ignored it and kept eating. After the fourth or fifth gummi, immediately she knew something was not right.

"Sky, I need to talk to you right quick."

When Sky turned around and looked at Amara, she already knew what she was about to say.

"Amara enjoy, relax, and have fun."

Amara knew that Sky had set her up again, before she could protest though Kevin started rubbing her back. She started feeling things she couldn't explain. All of the sudden Kevin started looking more and more like the movie stars she fantasized about at night. Sky must have been feeling great too, she was all over Jonathan and Amara just knew what was going to happen when they got to the hotel.

Finally they got to the hotel and took the elevator up to the penthouse suite. Amara was amazed when she saw the room. What was shocking is that it was not many other people there. Jonathan and Sky immediately disappeared. Kevin led her over to a huge chair where she sat down and couldn't resist the urge to lay back.

"Kevin can you get me something to drink please, my mouth is dry."

"Sure thing, make yourself comfortable."

Amara felt her heart racing but she couldn't move anymore once she laid back. She didn't know that the gummi bears not only had weed but they also had ecstasy in them. Kevin and Jonathan were really good kids, they just came from a family where doing drugs was the norm when it came to having fun.

Sky had told Jonathan that she smoked on the regular and popped pills when partying, so Kevin naturally though since Amara was with her she did the same thing. He would later feel horrible when he found that tonight was her first time doing any type of drugs.

Finding some white wine in the fridge, Kevin grabbed the bottles and wine glasses and headed back over to Amara. She had taken off her shoes and jeans, which brought a smile to his face.

"Amara here's your drink."

"Ohhhh wine, pretty."

"Pretty?"

"Yes look at the colors, LOOK!"

Kevin was entertained and fascinated at Amara's behavior. He knew that tonight was going to be fun, he would make sure to thank his brother later. Kevin scooted back in the chair with Amara and they just sipped on wine and talked. They were so into their conversation, that didn't notice that everyone had left when they noticed that Kevin and Jonathan were not going to party like usual.

Amara was shocked to find out that Kevin was a virgin and really wasn't thinking about sex. He had goals; being the star quarterback on the junior varsity football team, with a guaranteed spot on the varsity team next school year. Kevin knew that he would be a candidate for a full ride to colleges of his choice as long as he didn't get injured.

It was a comfortable silence when both stopped talking and just laid on the chair with their eyes closed. Sky's loud moaning and the bed could be heard as if the door was open. Kevin face started turning red with embarrassment, but Amara didn't budge.

"Amara...Amara!" Kevin was whispering why tapping her arm.

Fear set in when he noticed that Amara's chest was barely moving up and down. Kevin got up and started shaking her body and hollering her name. Still getting no response, he pulled out his phone and dialed 911. Then he went to the room and didn't even bother to knock, he just kicked the door open.

THE SEARCH FOR AMARA

Ignoring the fact that Sky was on top of his brother, he shouted that Amara was non-responsive and they needed to leave. He told his brother that the ambulance and then the police would be showing up soon. He warned Sky that she should stay with her friend, but she wasn't trying to hear that. She pulled on her clothes, and almost beat them out of the door. Jonathan was the playboy of the brothers. He hadn't really planned on talking to Sky after tonight anyway, but after this he knew he wouldn't be talking to her. Then again he had to think about it, because he had never experienced sex like he had with her. He had a hookup on fake IDs, so he didn't have to worry about the room coming back to him. Kevin had never prayed in his life, actually he barely knew anything about God. Words started pouring out of his mouth though, that if God was real could he please spare Amara's life and let their paths cross again. He had finally found a girl that he likes that was as ambitious as he was, and wasn't looking for a free ride on his dreams. The brothers hurried up and got on the elevator to leave. Kevin couldn't believe that Sky had ran and left her friend. He took one last look as the elevator door closed. When they reached the lobby, the paramedics were running in stopping at the front desk to get the key so they could access the penthouse. Kevin and Jonathan knew the ins and outs of the hotel, so they turned in the opposite direction to be sure that they weren't spotted by anyone that might remember their faces. They walked out of the hotel, trying their hardest not to take off running.

Chapter Twenty-Seven

The paramedics were not sure what to expect when they entered into the room.

"Hello, we got a call. Is anyone still here?"

The paramedics split up and went to search the room to see if anyone still needed their assistance.

"Over here!"

They met at the chair where Amara was lying with very shallow breathing. Her vitals were checked and then an oxygen mask was placed on her face. Then they put her on the stretcher to get her back downstairs and to the hospital quickly.

Amira's blood pressure was extremely low and dropping. Judging by her appearance, the hotel room setting, and her vitals the paramedics determined that she was probably experiencing a drug overdose or a life-threatening reaction to a drug.

One paramedic climbed behind the wheel, turned on the sirens and sped off into traffic. The other one couldn't do much in the back besides start the IV and monitor her until they reached the emergency room; he was heartbroken because he had a daughter around this age that had been acting out lately.

Responding to this call put things in perspective for him; as soon as his shift was over he was going home to talk to his family. This could be his daughter. He wondered where was her family, friends, or even the people she was with at the hotel.

THE SEARCH FOR AMARA

The ambulance turned into the hospital with the ER crew standing by. The doors opened and the crew whisked Amara off to the back. The paramedic informed the nurses that they had no info on the 'Jane Doe' that had come in. He told them that the case was personal and he would be coming back to the hospital when his shift was over to check up on her.

***

Sky made it back home and felt like she was about to pass out. She sat at the table and was constantly drinking glass after glass of water. Her mouth was so dry. She felt horrible about leaving Amara but she had freaked out and didn't know what to do.

She had now of getting in contact with anyone to let them know that Amara was in the hospital. She was getting scared because she couldn't stop feeling extremely thirsty and her heart was racing. Her phone started ringing in her back pocket which made her jump so hard she fell on the floor. Trying to get herself together she saw the call was coming from Taj.

"Hello."

"Sky what the hell happened to Amara?"

"What are you talking about?"

"There is a picture on Facebook of her looking dead, you are tagged in it!"

"I'll call you back."

Sky ended the call and opened the Facebook app. She had four friend requests, five inboxes, and forty-seven notifications. She went to her page so she could see the picture she was tagged in without having to go through the notifications. Sure enough it was a picture of Amara with her eyes closed looking like she was dead lying on the chair that was in the sitting area of the penthouse suite. The crazy thing was it looked like someone had created a fake page to be able to post the pic and tag her in it. It had to be Kevin or Jonathan, but then she remembered there were a couple of other people at the party. She sent Taj a text asking her to please tell Dontay to contact Amara's grandmother. Then she tried to call Jonathan one more time, but he was not answering so she turned her phone off. Climbing up the stairs to get in her bed, she hoped that when she went to sleep that she would wake up in the morning feeling better. She also prayed that Amara was doing much better.

CHAPTER TWENTY-EIGHT

Amara's picture on Facebook had sparked much chaos. Everyone was trying to figure out what was going on. Everyone just knew that Sky would have some answer since she was tagged in the picture. There were so many different rumors and speculations going around. Everything from Amara was dead to she was on life support to Sky and Amara were both in a coma.

Dontay was going crazy trying to get in touch with someone who knew what had really happened and where Amara was at. He had called Grandma Alicia, but didn't get an answer so he was waiting for her to call back.

Dontay started calling hospitals to see if they had Amara or a Jane Doe. He was not getting any success, until he called the last hospital. They said they had a Jane Doe that fit the description he gave. He hung up and called Grandma Alicia praying that she or Henry would pick up so that he would be able to see Amara when he got to the hospital.

"Hello."

"Momma Alicia, thank God you are finally home! Don't leave, I'm coming over."

"Is everything alright?"

"I will explain when I get there."

Dontay pressed end as he was running out the house. Common sense would have had him hop in the car, but his adrenaline had him run three blocks. When he got to the house Amara's grandparents and her mom were all standing outside with sad looks on their faces.

His heart dropped because he knew that they must have already received the news.

"Umm hello everybody."

"What information do you have Dontay?"

"I don't have much, except I did find out what hospital she is at."

"Great, because that is more information than what we have. I received a phone call from Lace screaming that she found out on Facebook that her cousin was dead. I had no idea what she was talking about until she sent me the picture. I am sick of this; I thought my daughter was at Sky's house."

"I told you that it was too early to let her be hanging back over her friend's house, but nooooo! Yo--"

"Mom now is not the time for I told you so, Dontay what hospital is my daughter at?"

"She is at St. Joseph's Children's."

"Well let's go see what is going on with my child."

Asha walked to the car, pissed that her mother would really say something like that at a time like this. They had no idea if Amara was going to live or die, and she wanted to worry about decisions that she had made as a mother.

THE SEARCH FOR AMARA

"Ms. Asha may I ride with you please" Dontay asked when he saw Momma Alicia and Henry get in the car and pull off.

This was the time that family needed to stick together and pray. Dontay just knew that they were going to pray together, but they left to go to the hospital. He could feel the hostility and it made him uncomfortable. He prayed a quick prayer to himself as they drove to the hospital.

***

The family sat in the waiting room where the nurses had instructed them to sit in and wait for the doctor. The television was on showing the news, but the sound was off and nobody was paying attention it anyways. Everyone was lost in their own personal thoughts. Dontay was just praying that Amara was okay, and he really wanted to know what had happened. Asha was thinking that all this was her fault; if she had just paid more attention to her children Amara would not be laid up in the emergency room. Alicia was meditating and silently praying. She probably had the most guilt in the room. She felt she had dropped the ball with her daughter and her granddaughter. Henry knew that his granddaughter would be just fine; he wished he could have stayed home but his wife would never let that happen. She was all about appearances.

Hours had passed and everyone had dozed off except for Asha. She couldn't sit still any longer so she went to look for a nurse. Just as she got to the door, a tall dark young man opened it.

"Are you Amara's mother?"

"Yes I am."

Everyone started slowly waking up when they heard the voice.

"Ma'am please have a seat. I have some serious questions."

"I would rather stan--"

"Asha sit down and answer the doctor's questions."

Asha cut her eyes at her mother while biting the inside of her cheek. Her mother had really been getting on her nerves. Asha made sure to sit in the chair where her back would be facing her mother.

"Mrs…."

"Ms. Kennedy."

"Asha real--"

"Mother please, sheesh can you let him get started so I can go see MY child!"

"Yep, your child. My apologies doctor, please continue.""

Dr. Arlington looked back and forth between the women and was curious about what was really going on. He would focus on that later.

"I am Dr. Arlington; I am Amara's initial doctor. Well ok, so do you know what brought your daughter into the emergency room tonight?"

"No honestly I do not. I thought she was at a friend's house until I heard about and saw the horrific picture of her on

Facebook, looking dead. What do you mean by initial, how many will she have?"

"I was the first doctor to examine her, how many more that will see her depends on how long she stays here. Have you talked to the friend?"

"No sir, we haven't had a chance to yet."

"Ok are you aware that your daughter has been using multiple types of drugs?"

"Excuse me?"

"Ma'am I won't use a bunch of medical terms and big words that most people do not understand. Your daughter has ecstasy and marijuana in her system. Now while those are bad, reality is that it is normal for teens to come in the emergency room with those drugs in their system. What concerns my colleagues and I are the high amounts of Dinitrophenol or DNP."

"What the hell is that? And it is not normal for my child to have any drugs in her system!"

"I understand how you feel Ms. Kennedy. DNP is an industrial chemical used in pesticides; it is also used to manufacture explosives. It is sometimes still used in some diet pills, which is how we are thinking it got in Amara's system."

"My Lord Jesus!" escaped from Alicia's mouth before she could stop herself.

"Doctor Arlington, I am still not understanding what is going on?"

"I cannot give you a time frame, but it appears that Amara had been taking these diet pills for quite some time. It is amazing that she hasn't been had a cardiac episode or even died. As crazy as they may sound, her doing whatever she was doing tonight may have actually saved her life."

"Oh my goodness, are you serious?"

"Very serious, do you know where she may have been getting the pills from?"

It was time for Dontay to speak up. He wasn't certain, but more than likely that was what Amara had sent to his house a while back telling him that it was a surprise for her grandmother. He got up and went to sit next to Asha.

"Umm excuse me, I think I have a good idea how Amara was getting the pills?"

"Oh really, is that because she was getting them from you?" Asha asked with her voice laced with anger and sarcasm.

"No ma'am. She was using her credit card and ordering them online."

"WHAT?"

"I told you that a twelve year old had no reason to ever have a credit card in her possession."

Asha jumped up, she no longer cared that Alicia was her mother. This was the final straw. She marched over to her chair and got in her face.

"YOU NEED TO LEAVE!"

"I am not going anywhere, and you better get out of my face. I don't care how mad you are, you are still my child."

Asha turned back towards the doctor asking him to call security so that Alicia could escorted out. Henry just sat back in the chair not saying a word. Even though Asha was being a bit disrespectful, he understood. Now was not the time to keep pointing out Asha's parenting skills that Alicia didn't agree with.

"Fine, I will go get security myself."

Alicia got up before Asha could completely turn around to leave out the room.

"Little girl I sa--"

"Ladies, let's get some order back in the room. We are not pointing out flaws and faults. There is a very young girl back there in a coma, and--"

"COMA? What? Wait when were you going to tell us that Amara was in a coma?"

"After I got to the bottom of what is going on with her body. She is in a medically induced coma. Her body temp when she arrived was way above the average, a temp that 98% of people die from." "JESUS, JESUS, JESUS, Lord cover Amara in the precious blood! Lord please watch over her, and if it be in your will, heal her completely." Henry could not take anymore; he got up left before anybody even tried to stop him. "Well can I see her?" "Let me go check her vitals and talk to her nurse, and then I will come back and get you." Alicia had left out to go find Henry after she finally noticed he was gone. She could not believe that her daughter was being so disrespectful. She knew that some of the things she said to Asha were unnecessary, but Alicia needed her to realize how serious this was. Dwayne had been a gift and a curse in her daughter's life. He had took her out of her funk of never dating again, but then things went downhill and Asha was now just wondering through life with no set plan. Her confusion was causing Amara to act out, and search for attention in all the wrong places. Now she was lying in a hospital bed in a coma, and all they could do is pray.

CHAPTER TWENTY-NINE

The doctor had come and told Asha that right now she was the only one that could go back to see Amara. Since he had placed Amara in a coma, she had been moved to Intensive Care and visits where very limited. Dr. Arlington expressed the importance of Amara may being able to hear, so no negative talk was allowed.

Asha hugged him and thanked him so much for treating her child with so much love. When she went to pull away, she noticed he held on a little longer. She was not trying to get involved with anyone ever again, but she had to admit the doctor seemed to have his stuff in order.

A nurse directed Asha to the sink where all visitors had to wash their hands thoroughly before they could enter to keep down the germs. After she dried her hands she was buzzed back and directed to the room where her daughter was.

Asha almost screamed, she could not believe that her daughter was in this situation. You could not have paid her to believe that her precious Amara would get involved in drugs and almost die. After the shock started wearing off, she walked over to the side of the bed and grabbed her daughter's hand.

Asha started self-reflecting on what she had been doing for the past year, and how it was having a horrible effect on her daughter's life and behavior. It was time to get things in order. She realized she hadn't seen her son in almost a month. Snapping out of the depression she was about to slip in, she cried out and started praying.

Remorse hit her when she realized that she had not been to church, she hadn't been praying and she couldn't even begin to remember the last time she opened her Bible. She felt like she had lost her whole identity after she married Dwayne.

Asha this is not about you, she had to remind herself.

Smoothing Amara's thick hair down on her head, Asha leaned over and placed her lips on Amara's forehead and stayed there for a few moments. Tears were coming down her face, and spilling into Amara's hair.

"Lord please don't take my baby because of my careless choices. Lord spare her, and bring her back. I promise I will be the mother you called me to be, just please give us another chance to get it right."

The lights started flashing and the machine started beeping. Asha jumped up to go get the nurses, but they were already rushing in the room with the crash cart and ushering her out. She ran down the hall to the waiting room and fell to her knees.

Asha was screaming and speaking incoherently to Dontay, but really she was speaking in tongues begging God for another chance. Alicia heard the cries. She pushed the foolishness to the back of her mind and got down on the floor with her daughter. They sat in the middle of the floor rocking, praying, and crying.

THE SEARCH FOR AMARA

Dontay did not know what to do. He was so scared for his friend Amara and her family. This was the first time he had ever experienced something like this. So worried about the current situations he had forgot all about his phone until he heard the last voice he wanted to hear, especially in a time like this.

"Dontay we have been calling you forever! Where is your phone?" Taj asked while walking in the room with her crew.

"Taj what are you doing here?"

"Huh, now you know Amara was my bestie!"

"Excuse me little girl, but this is not a damn party and my daughter is still alive so it is not was."

Taj's hand flew up to her mouth, "Oh I am so sorry, someone created a RIP Amara Facebook and a Go Fund Me Account, so how was I supposed to know," Taj said while flinging her hair over her shoulder.

"Wait does he have a video camera? GET OUT!"

"Taj you really need to leave, this is not the time or place. I will call you later," Dontay told her while shaking his head.

He had no plans on calling her later or ever again period. He could not believe that he was actually considering dealing with her. She had absolutely no class.

After she left, Alicia came over and talked to him. She let him know that they did not blame him for anything that happened. Then she issued a warning about girls like Taj, and how it would be beneficial for him in the long run to never deal with girls like her.

The doctor finally came to explain that Amara's body had suffered another cardiac episode, and they were packing her body with ice to try to break her temperature that kept spiking into very dangerous life-ending temps. The also had meds flowing through her veins to flush the drugs that were still in her system.

The family was in a waiting stage. Asha had been on the phone checking on DJ and calming down Lace at the same time. Delilah kept telling Asha that Lace would be ok if she could just see Amara. Asha disconnected the call and powered her phone off because she was tired of telling Delilah that Lace couldn't see Amara right now.

***

Late night, early morning Dr. Arlington came and got Asha asking her to come with him. Everyone was sleep so it was easy to sneak out. He led her down a quiet dark hallway that didn't look like it was even in use.

"Asha I know that this is a very inappropriate time to be thinking about this, but I don't want to risk missing out on my blessing. Would it be possible for us to keep in touch, once Amara is released?"

"Ummm my luck with relationships is horrible, so I don't think that would b...wait did you just say when Amara is released?"

"Yes has been monitored for the past few hours, and if her vitals remain constant she will be getting moved to a regular room. Once the test results come back negative which usually takes a couple of days she will be discharged."

"OH MY GOODNESS!" Asha screamed while jumping up and down.

Dr. Arlington took the opportunity to grab her and give her the kiss he had wanted to give her since he first laid eyes on her. Her response though was unexpected when she slapped him so hard his ears started ringing.

"Are you freaking crazy?"

"I'm sorry Ms. Kennedy"

"Yes you are sorry, is this how you get dates? Take me to my daughter."

"No it is not, you have to know I have never done anything like this before. Again I apologize and I will come get you as soon as Amara is placed in a room."

He quickly exited the hallway and jogged over to the elevator full of embarrassment. Asha shook her head, looked up and started thanking God all over again as she made her way back to her family.

When she entered the room everyone was still asleep except her father.

"Hey daddy."

"Hey is everything ok, you look a little disturbed."

Asha stopped herself before she told her father what had just happened. She knew he would go find Dr. Arlington and give him a beat down along with a lot of threats. Instead she told him the good news about Amara. "I was never worried about Amara. Yes she has made some very stupid choices, but she come from a family of warriors so I knew she would bounce back. Now we just have to get back to our war training to make sure she doesn't slip again." "You are absolutely right Henry, get back to being that family that prays together," Alicia said with her eyes still closed. Asha looked around at everyone in the room and realized that these were the people that truly cared about Amara and it was time to tighten up the circle. Dontay was now considered as much family as if he shared their bloodline. He came over and hugged Asha while sitting down next to her. Everyone grabbed his hands, and Henry started praying.

CHAPTER THIRTY

They had got Amara moved to her room and she had drifted in and out of sleep the whole time. In her mind it was the next day, but she had missed out on an entire day. She knew that she was in the hospital but she had no idea why. She couldn't remember anything besides walking to the park with Sky.

Sky had been adamant about meeting some white boys and going to a hotel party. Amara remembered have a bad feeling about going but letting Sky convince her that they would have fun. Staring up at the ceiling, she was really trying to determine how long had she been laying here.

She rolled over to push the call button, but the door opened before she could find the remote. Her mother and a tall man that was obviously the doctor walked in the room. If he didn't have on a lab jacket and a stethoscope around his neck, Amara would have thought that her mother had a new boyfriend already.

"Hi honey, how are you feeling?"

Amara wished that she could have played sleep. Her mother was acting calm now, but she knew there would be a lot of questions to be answered that truthfully she did not have answers to.

"Okay."

"Amara I am sure that you are uncomfortable, but I am not going to sugarcoat because of the severity of this situation."

Amara got extremely nervous and glanced back and forth between her mother and the doctor.

"Amara you had three different types of drugs in your system and you almost died. We had to put your body in a medically induced coma to drop your temperatures. Can you tell us what happened? Don't try to save your friends because they were not worried about saving you! They left you to die alone in a hotel room."

Amara started shaking and crying. She couldn't believe what the doctor had just told her and because of her past behavior, nobody was going to believe that she really could not remember.

"Amara did you hear what he said?" Asha asked.

She glanced up at her mother with tears in her eyes and a look of confusion. The recently turned thirteen year old girl was realizing that she had no clue what she getting into when she made decisions to act like an adult. Closing her eyes she was trying very hard to remember something, but absolutely nothing was coming back to her memory. "Amara!" the doctor called out. "Look I know that no one is going to believe this, but I do not remember. I know that sounds crazy. Maybe you can ask Sky, the last memory I have is being with her." Asha looked ashamed that her thirteen year old daughter was having this type of conversation. She shocked her daughter when she told her that no one had seen or heard from Sky. The doctor then told them, that the police had been waiting to speak to her and he was going to get them.

"Amara now is not the time to cover up for anyone. Did you hear him say that no one cared about you?" "Mom I am serious, I am not covering for anyone. I do not have any memories from what happened last night. I said ask Sky." "Amara calm down with that tone. First of all we have not been able to get in contact with Sky or her family. Of course we tried them first because that is where you were at! Secondly this happened the day before yesterday." "What? Are you serious?" "Yes, you were in a coma all day yesterday because you had a temperature of 105° and it kept rising." Before Amara could get another word out, the police officers entered the room. What a coincidence that it was the same officers that had arrested her not too long ago from the school. Asha spoke to the officers explaining that Amara did not have any memory of what had happened, and gave them Sky's information. The officers shocked both Asha and Amara when they explained that the room she was found in belonged to someone that had a fake ID and had rented out rooms in several hotels across the state of Florida. Usually the rooms would have girls left in them to be found the next day by housekeeping. The girls were never dead, but they were usually ganged raped and badly beaten and bruised. The fact that she had been taking diet pills that were deadly as well, had actually saved her life. They offered Asha a card of an excellent therapist that they recommended Amara should see. Asha just looked at her daughter in amazement and told her that she was going to get the rest of the family. When she left out,

Amara broke down in tears not knowing that her mother was on the other side of the door doing the same thing. When she got back to the waiting room, she was sad to see that Dontay had left. Alicia explained that he said Amara would probably be embarrassed and he would just visit her at home or another day if she requested his presence. Asha told her parents the room number and sat in one of the chairs. She laid her head back and stretched her feet out in a chair across from her finally able to get some rest. Just as she slipped into a relaxing sleep, she heard the door open and looked up into Dwayne's eyes. "I know you don't want to see me, but when Delilah called and told me what was going on I had to come see Amara. I hope you don't mind." "Not at all, you have to wait for my parents to come back out." Thoughts were going crazy in Asha's head but she blocked them out and just focused on resting. She didn't know why Dwayne had come, and she wanted to say something really mean about him and Melissa but she kept her mouth and her eyes closed. Dwayne realized that this was probably not a good time, so he got up and walked out.

EPILOGUE

It seemed like everyone had decided to send their kids out of the state. Amara finally was discharged to go home after three extra days. When she returned back to school she really felt like a celebrity. Everybody was going on and on about how they were so happy that she was not dead. Sky and Taj were both gone. No one knew where Sky was, but Taj's parents had sent her to live with an aunt was what Amara was told. Rumor had it though, that her parents had sent her to a detox center. When word got around that Amara had drugs in her system, parents started freaking out and paying attention to what they their kids were doing. Lace and Amara had been talking again like normal. Amara had even been Facetiming with Dwayne when Lace was over. The end of the school year was in two days and Amara could not believe how her first year of high school had played out. From standing up for herself, gaining an interest in boys and sex, sneaking out, partying, and almost dying, Amara knew she had better slow down. Being only thirteen, she had a long life ahead of her with a lot she planned to accomplish. Knowing that she almost died, she swore she would never ever touch drugs again. She didn't even want to take a Tylenol. Dontay would come around every once in a while, but he was very distant which was fine with Amara because she was swearing off boys. Well that she was telling herself, but she no idea what the next school year would bring. Would she be able to stick to her word? Find out in the next story…..

Made in the USA
Charleston, SC
04 June 2016